BEFORE CLOSURE

A novel by Shadley Grei

Before Closure

ISBN:

978-1-965629-00-0 (paperback)

978-1-965629-06-2 (e-book)

Cover, interior design and illustrations by Timothy J. Prough

Published by Kingbird Press
kingbirdpress.com

Printed in the United States of America
First Edition

For the ones who calm me down,

And the ones who crack me up.

And for Dave,

All the muches.

"There will be a sea of tears,

You'll gasp for your breath at times,

You'll drag your heavy heart

And drown your soul in the sea.

But sooner or later,

The sea will dry up,

There won't be any savior ship

But you'll learn to embrace

The wet sand revealed."

– Sanhita Baruah

"Closure is bullshit."

– James Ellroy

PROLOGUE

Before.

She had misplaced her life and needed to find it while it was still of use to her.

Her hand wasn't even shaking as she wrote the letter. She was crying but refused to let her tears hit the page, instead dabbing her eyes with the sleeve of her silk shirt. The tears would stain this shirt, one of her favorites, and that was okay. That was what she wanted. The stains like little silken scars.

They would not understand. How could they? She barely understood the decision herself, and she was the one making it. She knew it was cruel, but there was something about the brutality that she needed as well. That was the darkest secret, the masochistic thrill of the jolt only cruelty can bring.

She emptied the smaller of her two jewelry boxes, the one that held her everyday wear. She looked in the bigger box, the one protecting the special pieces—her mother's pearls, the pendant from her mother-in-law, the diamond earrings for special occasions. The only piece she took was tucked at the bottom, the simple bracelet of two birds, their wings built from the birthstones of her children. She looked around the room and felt the pull of the bed to rest until the desire passed, but she had to fight it. She knew what she had to do.

How many times had she considered doing this, especially once the children left home? It had nothing to do with a lack of love for her husband. She has felt secure in his love since the moment he said hello. But a security blanket can still smother you. She wanted to be content. God knows the number of times she'd spent staring at herself in the mirror, willing herself to settle the call to run. What kind of monster could smile through the comfort of the life she'd built for her family, only to feel herself screaming on the inside to go? To explore? To find out what might be waiting on the other side of this brutal decision, this unforgivable act of abandonment? The time would come when she would look back on this moment with regret. That she did not doubt.

Even so, her hand did not shake.

She had wandered through the house for days, deciding where she would leave this note. She had even set empty envelopes in various places and left the room, only to return to see how it looked. Should it wait on the desk in the hall? Rest against the dusty picture frame holding a family memory? Stand amongst the collection of prescription bottles?

It wasn't until she finished writing what she had to say and signed her name to the bottom that she forwent the envelope altogether. Instead, she left it on the kitchen counter, using a coffee mug made by her son as a paperweight. She dropped the pen into the mug and stared at it until all shapes melted into watercolor edges, and the life she was standing in started to feel like a memory.

Her tears had stopped by the time she reached the two bags she had left by the back door. She knew the crying wasn't over, but that the staying was.

And she left.

FRIDAY

1

EGGS.

FRANKIE IS IN A PITCH-BLACK freefall. His jaw feels locked tight, and he has the distinct feeling that if he tries to scream, his face might explode and send his teeth scattering like confetti into the abyss.

He's pretty sure he's dreaming—or nightmaring, as it were—but at this point, who can say for sure?

Suddenly, a song comes from the void, sounding like an aria for a dying Disney princess. His curiosity about the source of the song replaces his fear of falling. He tips his head to try to locate the source, which wakes him up. He finds he is, in fact, falling. The song is the ringtone reserved for his sister, and he's falling out of bed while reaching for his phone in his sleep.

His arm slams against the nightstand and sends a half-empty water bottle chasing his keys and melatonin gummies across the room. He manages to click on the speakerphone just as he faceplants on the floor. The bounce of his body brings his phone crashing down on the back of his head, where it slides down to rest against his neck. Turning his head to it, he flips it onto its back.

"Hello," he groans.

His sister, Jules, is oblivious to what has occurred. She also seems oblivious that she called him, as he can hear her reprimanding someone.

"So, that's the same reason I gave you the last time. You don't need to do that. Just hit the—"

He hears the 'ting-ting' of cash register buttons, followed by the 'clack-whoosh' of the drawer opening. He imagines her standing behind the counter at his coffee shop, Fuel Injector, with the phone tucked under her chin. She probably has her hair pulled back with a twist tie and a razor blade smile as she once again tells one of the staff how to work the register. Although he owns Fuel Injector, he hasn't set foot behind the counter since the day his mother left. Jules offered to cover while Frankie took some time off to handle everything that happened in the aftermath. Neither of them expected that seven months later, she'd still be the one behind the counter.

She isn't speaking to him and perhaps her frustration with whomever she's talking to has caused her to forget that she'd called him. He starts to hang up but pauses when he hears her say, "Eggs."

He considers hanging up anyway to make some kind of point, but he doesn't.

"What?"

Jules huffs under the burden of needing to elaborate. "Eggs. We need eggs. Bring me four dozen on your way to the job you should quit so you can get back here where you belong."

Frankie sits up to brace himself for her response to what he's about to say. "I'm taking a sick day."

He can almost hear her blood boil up to the back of her eyes as she struggles to swallow expletives in front of her customers. Instead, she uses a much cruder alternative: mom voice. "Frankie, sweetie. I know you're having a hard time, but we all are. This didn't just happen to you, okay? So, pull on your big boy pants, get in your big boy car, and bring me some eggs. Got it? Thanks. Byeeeeeeeee."

The line goes dead, and he contemplates her reaction if he ignores her and goes back to bed until something, anything, feels like it makes sense again. He savors the glorious imagery of her head exploding like a cartoon. For some sick reason, this gives Frankie the energy to drag himself off the floor.

He stretches and feels a small pop at the base of his neck, which kicks his vision and knocks him off balance.

Almost 40 feels different from what he expected. Younger. Older. Wiser. Dumber. He's months behind on buzzing the scrappy hair that he will always consider blond. Truth is, it darkened and thinned and invited in some gray years ago that usually hide below a tight buzz cut. His beard also needs some attention. The scruffy handsomeness he's usually going for has given way to shaggy hobo. His broad shoulders slump, and he's reminded of an old bit by comedian Paula Poundstone. He stretches up to arch his back a little as he remembers her saying from her hunched-over perch on a stool, "If I were on Sesame Street, I would represent the letter 'O.' " She also once observed that her father looked like a potato standing on toothpicks. Frankie didn't think he was there yet, but the hand resting on his belly suggested he may be closer than he'd like.

He stretches again, releasing a chorus of snap-crackle-farts through his joints that sounds like a bag of gravel dropped in a blender. It makes him laugh, and he mumbles, "Getting older isn't kid's stuff."

Jules' voice still lingers in his head—sharp, tense—and something about the call makes him restless.

He looks around his childhood bedroom. This hasn't officially been his room for 20 years. Though his mother converted it to a more formal guest room when he didn't move home after college, he can still see a thousand memories peeking at him from every corner. Struck with random curiosity, he grabs his phone and asks Siri how many days are in 18 years. The clipped voice comes back, "18 years is 6,574.36 days."

He thanks the robot, as is his habit, and looks around again, asking no one but the dust bunnies, "What the hell is point three-six of a day?"

Over 6,500 mornings started with him in this exact spot. The bed has never moved. It's forever tucked in this nook next to the window with the bookcase headboard. He looks up at that bookcase now and pulls down a picture of himself at eight or nine, sitting in a tire swing in the backyard. He looks like a happy child, which doesn't compute with the childhood he remembers. His childhood was fine. Probably great by many standards, but he was a miserable child. "Miserable" isn't the word. Melancholy, maybe? Depressed, for sure. Even when things were going well, or even great, it was always his nature to become sad about how the good times inevitably end. He never knew where this emotion came from, as the rest of his family seemed genuinely joyful. Or maybe happy is just the face that everybody sells.

Perhaps that disconnect explains why his mother left seven months ago, leaving behind only a letter Frankie's father had refused to let Frankie or Jules read. "It wasn't addressed to you," their father's only justification. Frankie didn't feel like thinking about it or the chain reaction that followed, which led him to wake up in his childhood room all these months later. He never felt like thinking about it, which was probably part of the reason he was stuck in it. You can't process what you don't acknowledge.

He looks again at the nightstand. Under the globs of melatonin is a reminder he'd written on the back of a daily affirmation page-a-day calendar that he'd turned into scratch paper. In his nearly illegible penmanship were the words, "Get over it."

He raises his middle finger to the piece of paper and glances over at the suitcase propped open on an old dresser. He painted the dresser black during the dark period that started in his mid-teens and continues to this day. With the way the morning shadows hit the open suitcase, it looks like a Jim Henson creation, a gap-mouthed Muppet, begging Frankie to do exactly that. *Get over it.* But he isn't sure how. His mother's exit had torn through so many of the lies that kept him upright that he was still trying to remember how to walk all these months later.

He glances at his phone, again contemplating calling in sick, but he notices the time instead. He has a good two hours before he has to leave for work. Lately, he's challenged the number of times he can hit the snooze button before actually starting the day, but today, thanks to his asshole sister, he was wide awake with time to spare. He glances at the window and can see that the morning light is just beginning to crack open the day here in Iowa, so he does something he hasn't done in months. He pulls on his sweatpants and work boots and heads out for a walk in the fields.

The morning is already warm, hinting at another July scorcher. Frankie's boots crunch on the gravel as he passes the barn, veering off the path and into the rows of towering corn.

The field stretches out in every direction, the corn swaying gently in the breeze, the rolling hills in the distance. Sometimes he forgets how beautiful this land can be. Their land. These 1,200 acres on the outskirts of Des Moines have been in the family for three generations.

Frankie and Jules are the last of the line. They grew up on this farm, helped their dad with chores, lived the rural life. But neither of them is cut out for it. They've agreed to sell the place once their dad can't handle it anymore, and though that decision is settled, it doesn't sit right with Frankie this morning.

He imagines keeping the farm, running it himself. It's not realistic, not the life he ever wanted, but there's something sweet about the fantasy. He used to picture it differently, back when Shane was in the picture. They'd talked about staying here, growing old on the porch, watching Shane's kids play in the fields, passing the farm down to another generation.

That future's gone, but it still haunts him, lingering like a ghost on the edges of his thoughts.

His boot sinks into a patch of wet mud, and he swears under his breath. He tries to pull his foot free, but the mud grips tighter, and with one last yank, his foot slips out of the boot entirely. He stumbles forward, his sock landing square in the cold, wet muck.

"Shit," he mutters, staring down at the mess.

He just stands there for a moment, his sock squelching in the mud, the absurdity of it all washing over him. It's not lost on him that even the weakest of minds would see this as the perfect metaphor for his whole life—constantly trying to push forward, only to get stuck.

He manages to pull his boot out and shoves his foot back in, though his sock is already soaked. With a sigh, he turns back toward the house, avoiding the deeper patches of mud this time.

As he reaches the yard, he spots his aunt, Matches, and her husband, Pete, near the chicken coop, chatting with their backs to him. The last thing he needs is a conversation right now, so he ducks behind the coop, slipping around the side.

He's almost past when one of the hens lets out a loud squawk, pecking at his boot. Frankie hisses under his breath and sidesteps the bird, hurrying toward the kitchen door.

The smell of coffee hits him as soon as he steps inside, the familiar warmth of it pulling him out of his thoughts. The coffee pot is already half full—someone's started it before him, either Matches or his dad. He pours himself a cup and leans against the counter, listening to the quiet hum of the house. It feels too quiet, too still. The kind of silence that makes you think of everything you don't want to.

Voices outside pull his attention to the window. There, he finds Matches and Pete moving along the massive garden. Matches hides from the morning sun under an enormous straw sunhat, her signature long silver-blond braid snaking down her willowy back. She has two baskets of onions halfway down her lane while Pete crawls along the next row over, a few feet behind her, with a bin full of carrots. Several feet behind them, Pete's sliver of a grandson, JP, struggles to survive the oppressive labor. He is thirteen. Isn't that punishment enough?

Frankie watches them for a moment. It's not yet 7:00 am, but the late July heat is already steaming the earth. Sweat soaks through Pete's shirt as he reaches over to swipe the hat from Matches's head to fan them both. He can't pick up their conversation through the window over the low hum of the air conditioner, but he can hear them laugh as they talk. Well, Matches and Pete laugh. JP is incapable. Again, he's thirteen. It's not his fault.

Back upstairs, Frankie pauses at his father's bedroom door and prepares to knock. In the weeks following his mother's vanishing act, Frankie found himself in this same place every morning. He'd raise his hand to knock on his father's door, only to pause. For a while, the recurring pause confused him until he realized the reason. He feared that one morning, he would discover his father was gone, too. Perhaps he died in his sleep. Perhaps the grief ended with a handful of sleeping pills. Perhaps he left to find the leaving kind. The pause before knocking is how Frankie's heart prepares for whatever comes next.

He knocks and starts to count. At some point, he had decided if he ever got to 10, it meant his father was gone, in whatever way he was going to go.

Sometimes, his father opens the door on the count of two, fully dressed and ready for the day. But this morning, it took a while. Frankie stops counting when he gets to seven. He also stops breathing until he hears a soft "Morning, Frankie" from the other side of the door.

He pushes the door open and finds his father lying fully dressed on the bed, which is made military tight. Clayton William Parker, Jr. wears dust-stained jeans and a white tank top, revealing how his former muscled stockiness has started to fade with time, like most of his hair. He's handsome, which makes Frankie less afraid of getting older, if this is what his future self might look like. Some days Clayton looks frailer than others, but today, he looks rested, farmer-fit, and clean-shaven. Though he looks good, Frankie still scans his memory. Is this what his father was wearing when he headed to bed? Perhaps he slept in his clothes, if he slept at all?

Clayton, as a father can do, seems to read Frankie's mind. "I already showered. I'm just gathering my energy before I face Matches this morning. Sometimes there's not enough coffee in the world…"

Frankie smiles, and the tear that leaps to the edge of his eyelashes surprises him. Something is unsettling about seeing his father lying like this on his bed. He looks both fragile and indestructible. Like the rest of us, Frankie's father was an hourglass filled with broken dreams and burning time. Frankie longs to say something careful and wise.

"I'm taking Jules some eggs," isn't it, but it'll have to do.

"Is she paying for them?"

It's the same question every time. And the same answer. "Yes, she's paying for them. With love."

Clayton considers this for a moment, and Frankie watches him think. Frankie wonders what they might say to each other if all the walls between them fell away. They're not distant, but they're not close. They circle the middle ground where love lives in the silence. Clayton is a wonderful, generous, and kind father, but he is also a countryman in his 60s. He's not an ocean of emotional vulnerability. And Frankie started hiding parts of himself the minute he realized he was more interested in the jocks than the cheerleaders. Even after coming out, some things still felt safer unsaid. So, they became men—father and son—who loved each other as best they could from opposite sides of fear.

"You better get down there," Frankie says. "If Matches finishes a row before you show up, you'll never hear the end of it."

Clayton sighs. "I've known that woman for 62 years. I have yet to hear the end of it."

Frankie smiles at his father's laughter and gives the nod shared between men to say what words can't. He continues toward the shower, hoping to wash away his apprehension of another day.

2

CRACKS.

THERE'S A CRACK IN THE WALL above where Frankie had been standing. It has created a dark, jagged river in the ceiling that extends into the pale yellow wallpaper covered in pastel roses. Carol had selected this wallpaper right after they moved in, and it had remained flawless until the day she left. Had she slammed the door before leaving? Or was it cracked before, and he hadn't noticed? Is it proof of his inability to notice things, as Carol had been keen to mention? Is it an omen? A sign?

Or maybe it's just a fuckin' crack in the ceiling.

He grumbles at the thought, unhappy to hear the curse word, even in his head. He doesn't consider himself a prude, but he has, for many years, prided himself on being able to get his point across without the need to curse. Lately, these words have skidded across his psyche with more frequency.

At 65, he has convinced himself that life had few surprises

left to give him. He isn't so arrogant as to think he has it all figured out, but he had nestled into the belief that he was, at the very least, semi-prepared for whatever might happen.

This belief became a sandcastle in a hurricane on January 7th when his wife of 39 years left without warning. There wasn't even an envelope around the bombshell built from 237 words. Somehow, this seemed the cruelest part, that she didn't seem to care that anyone could have found the note. That's one thing he'd have to mention when she returned. She was coming back, of course. She always did when she went off on these adventures. And he was already dreading the uncomfortable conversations they'd need to have about the way she left. The "I feel" statements always sounded more like "you should."

He sits up on the edge of the bed and presses his feet into the floor as if trying to crush the desire to curse her.

He stands up and enters the tiny, private bathroom just a few feet from the bed. This had been one of Carol's requests during the last renovation. Funny that she had waited until the kids had left the house to ask for a private bathroom. There were only two of them. What privacy did she need? Apparently, more than he had realized.

The things she left behind stare at him with more questions than answers. A tiny bowl of earrings. Expired migraine medication. A bobby pin in the soap dish. Sometimes, he talks to them as if they can transport his messages to Carol. This morning, he shakes hands with the pink bathrobe hanging on the back of the door. It has been a challenging few months, and he's grateful that the break is ending. She'll be back on Sunday. He's sure of it, regardless of the surrounding whispers. It's their anniversary, after all. Forty years of marriage. Three more days and then the healing, the fixing, the plastering together of their splintered relationship can begin again. They've done it before, though she's never been gone this long.

He chokes down his morning pills until he realizes he's holding a cup of water, and he takes a sip, shaking his head. He feels himself think, "It's gonna be one of those days," but spits it out with his mouthwash. Slipping on his favorite navy blue overshirt, he heads down to the kitchen for a second cup of coffee before facing his sister. As had become his standard operating procedure these days, he'd been up before the sun and had his first cup of coffee while still in his robe. Most mornings, he'd find himself on the porch in the rocking chair his father had made. The one that sits next to the one Clayton had made for Carol. A cup of coffee with the ghost of his wife, then a shower to rinse off his confusion, then another cup before facing the day. This morning, however, he forgot to stop for his second cup. Already outside, he freezes on the back step and wonders if he should go back in. He is now at an equal distance from his coffee cup and the garden. Perhaps the fact that he forgot to stop in the kitchen means he knows he doesn't need it. Or, perhaps, his memory has packed up to go, not bothering to leave an open letter on the counter before exiting.

The uncertainty of this very banal moment frustrates Clayton, and he uses it as an excuse to crouch down and pull weeds from the flowerbed by the back door. He finds a cigarette butt tucked under the burgundy star petunias, and he wonders if Frankie has started smoking again. It wouldn't be surprising. They should all be smoking. Or, at the very least, setting things on fire.

He tucks the evidence in his shirt pocket and looks up to see Matches and Pete cross the yard where Frankie is loading eggs into the back of his minivan. Seeing his sister with Pete is always surprising, mostly because of how the past and the present tango in his mind. Pete and Clayton have been friends since grade school, and a big part of their childhood was tormenting Clayton's little sister, Margaret Ann. They tortured her dolls, stuck gum in her pigtails, and switched sugar with salt in her "sweet tea." Somehow, Margaret Ann refused to be deterred, instead seeing these tortures as tests she always passed. She was faster and braver than both Pete and Clayton combined. She was the first kid in their crew to climb the city water tower, jump from Tassel Ridge Bridge, and explore the drainpipes below the unattended and open manhole. Pete and Clayton pretended to be cool, but Margaret Ann was the real deal. Not that they'd ever admit it.

As teenagers, they'd all sneak out with classmates and young neighbors to party on the edge of farmer Slawson's property. They'd take beers they had slipped from their father's coolers and bottles they had lifted from part-time jobs in grocery stores and gas stations. Pete and Clayton would show up sometimes, with Margaret Ann arriving moments later, following them on her pink bike. Clayton would tell her to go home, and she would threaten to tell Mama and Daddy where they were. She didn't drink, but she liked to be around the older kids, and some boys liked to have her around, especially as her body started leaving childhood behind. Clayton and Pete had to step in more than once when it seemed like someone, namely Dale Blackford, was getting too friendly. Not that Margaret Ann needed protecting. When she was 13, Dale had taken her by the hand to lead her back to where the bad boys "talked" to good girls, but Margaret Ann wasn't one to go where she didn't want to go. She used her free hand to grab a book of matches tucked in Dale's shirt pocket and somehow lit the entire matchbook against his chest. As his shirt ignited and he ran screaming for the Slawson pond, Margaret Ann casually returned to the group and took part in the game of tossing toads through an old tire swing while Dale threw himself into the water to stop the flames. That incident became a legend that few believed unless they were there. It's also how Margaret Ann became "Matches" and, 10 years later, Mrs. Dale Bickford.

At their wedding, Dale Blackford joked that Margaret Ann had literally burned herself into his heart, not to mention his flesh, on that fateful day. They were comfortably, if not always happily, married for 32 years until cancer came to plant itself in their lives. What everyone assumed was lower back pain from 40 years of Dale working the farm was instead the notification that a spinal tumor had crashed their party. This began the next chapter of their lives together. All of Matches's childhood strength and bravery would be called upon to help Dale make the journey to the end of his life.

During one of Dale's better days, Matches surprised him with a party back on the edge of the Slawson's farm, which had survived suburban sprawl. This party had to happen across the street from a new Super Target, but party they did. Clayton invited Pete along, hoping it might lift his spirits after a divorce that had gone from civilized to "see you in hell."

In Dale's sickness, Pete found a place where he could be useful in the shadow of his difficult divorce and early retirement. Pete came around often and was in Matches's house when Dale died. Matches laid down with Dale to whisper her goodbyes and to wish him safe travels on his journey through the light. As this happened, Pete sat in the kitchen, making newspaper butterflies from a stack left by the back door. His grandson, JP, had learned to make them in his art class at school and had shown Pete how to do it. This silly little skill kept Pete's mind from splitting into a thousand pieces as he listened to Matches send Dale into the next world.

Matches came out of the bedroom to find 121 paper butterflies tucked in all corners of her kitchen. Teary and newsprint-stained, Pete reminded Matches she was not alone. She didn't realize that Pete needed her to remind him of the same thing. One year later, they were married. When Carol left, it took two days for Clayton to tell Matches and Pete. It was impossible to turn the confusion into words, especially for a man who doesn't like to acknowledge the fragile pieces that live in the cage of his chest. In fact, he never actually told them. He guessed that they had heard from Frankie or Jules. One morning in late January, he woke to the sound of distant conversation in the yard. He raced to the window, hoping, expecting to see Carol bundled in her winter coat, scattering seeds to the chickens. Instead, he found Matches and Pete removing the last of the Christmas lights from the bushes and shoveling a path from the patio to the barn. Seeing them there, working, and getting on with it, reminded him that he had to get back to living while waiting for Carol's return. She'd rather come back to his corpse than find him lazy and sad. So, he pulled on his work boots. He didn't want to explain, and he didn't have to. Somehow, Matches just knew. Matches always knew.

Besides, he had Franklin and Julie to think about. Even adults are children. He felt bad because he hadn't been able to give Jules much focus during these last few months, not with how Frankie's life fell apart after Carol left. Clayton wondered if Carol would have made a different decision if she realized what her choice was going to do to Frankie's life, relationship, and family.

When Clayton found Carol's letter, he called Frankie and Jules to tell them their mother had left town for a few months. They drove out to the house and asked to read the letter, but he told them no. If Carol had wanted them to read it, she would have addressed it to them. She was gone for a while. That's all they needed to know. So, Frankie and Jules spent the night in their childhood rooms, and then Jules returned to her husband, Damon, and daughter, Sophie. Frankie, always taking on more than he should, stayed a few days longer before returning to the family and life he was building with Shane. Frankie didn't know that he should have warned Shane he was coming back to his own house, because Frankie walked in on Shane with someone else. Apparently, Shane had cheated before, but Frankie had witnessed nothing until that day. The relationship imploded, so Frankie returned to the farm, where he was still waiting for all the broken pieces to heal.

Clayton believed Frankie was strong enough to survive the breakup with Shane. He wondered, though, if Frankie had the skills to process also losing Shane's kids. He saw how the loss clawed at Frankie whenever he saw other families, dads with kids. Being a stepdad had changed Frankie. Carol often talked about it. The way it settled his raging heart a bit. Clayton, not one to talk about emotions, would nod his head, but it made him happy to see a different light around Frankie.

Clayton tried to talk to his son a few times in the months since everything fell apart, but it felt uncomfortable. They needed Carol's soothing touch and words. Maybe when she returns, Frankie will heal for real.

From the back porch, Clayton watches Frankie slide the eggs into the back of his minivan, thinking maybe his son is more fragile than those delicate shells. Pete helps him balance the box while Matches asks him about work. Clayton can barely hear their conversation, but he imagines Frankie is trying to be cordial while also wanting to run away as fast as he can.

Clayton walks across the yard, wanting to rescue his son from the banality of casual conversation, reaching them just as Frankie closes the hatch on the van. JP joins them, popping into his mouth a few of the ripe blackberries from the bucket he carries. Clayton reaches out and messes with his hair. "JP, my boy, if you don't stop growing, you're gonna be taller than your grandpa."

JP almost smiles but shrugs instead, and Clayton turns to tease Pete. "God knows you're already better-looking."

Pete rolls his eyes and punches Clayton on the shoulder. "You don't need to be pretty when you're tough."

Matches pops off one of her glorious laughs. "Anymore, you're both tough as a box of bullshit."

Clayton glances at Frankie, whose gritted silence is begging for an exit. "Get on to work. You'll be late if you have to drop the eggs to Jules on your way."

Frankie smiles in gratitude for the out and heads toward the driver's door. "I'll be back at two o'clock."

Clayton shakes his head. "You don't need to do that."

Frankie sighs and comes back to him. "Tomorrow's the farmers' market. I'm coming back to help, okay? You need me here more than they need me dusting off a stack of years-old files. I already got it cleared."

Clayton can only smile at his insistence.

Out of nowhere, JP finally speaks up. "Where's Mrs. Parker?"

It's a casual question. But it lands like an icepick, and Clayton notices the S.O.S. look that passes between Frankie, Matches, and Pete.

"She's been gone for a few months," Clayton says. "But she's coming back on Sunday."

He ignores the way Matches's eyes widen while Frankie's body turns into a clenched fist. He looks like he might say something else but settles for, "I'll be back at two." He shakes his head and slides into the driver's seat, throwing his father the saddest smile before he heads down the driveway.

Clayton lets the silence sting for a bit, entertained by how JP tries to understand, before letting the air out of it all as he heads for the greenhouse. "I'll get the tomato pallets."

As he walks away, he overhears Matches saying, "For a kid that doesn't like to talk, you're certainly careless with the words you do say."

"What'd I do?"

Clayton slips into the greenhouse before hearing Matches's reply, which is for the best. It's too nice of a morning to fight.

3

COFFEE.

"UH, I'LL HAVE, LIKE, a large almond soy goddess latte and a vegan, gluten-free hempnola faux-nut muffin."

The girl looks 12, but that doesn't stop Jules from wanting to knock her down. She doesn't, but she imagines the offense in extraordinary detail as she puts the order together. It's not that she hates the stuff they make and sell; there are just days when the pretentiousness makes her hate the people who easily buy into it.

After giving the girl her plate, Jules watches her join her little group of friends at the table by the window. Their phones immediately swallow them up, and they disappear from each other. Her hand hovers over the option to shut off the Wi-Fi, something that "accidentally" happens occasionally. She considers it her gift-with-purchase to remind people they are more than their pocket selves. But she decides against it. Like many things, fantasy beats reality.

The reality of standing here at the west end of downtown Des Moines at here brother's cafe is a perfect example. After the one-two punch of their mother leaving and Shithead Shane cheating on Frankie, Frankie asked Jules to cover at Fuel Injector for a few days. She enjoyed helping over the years and welcomed the break from being a stay-at-home mom. She didn't realize that meant also saying yes to taking over the café full-time for several months while Frankie hid in a file room job at a company that makes farm equipment.

As she uses a twist tie to pull her bangs back from her eyes, the loose skin under her arm catches her eye, and she wrinkles her nose at the reminder of age. Not that she needed help to remember, thanks to a seven-year-old daughter who inherited both her iron will and blunt honesty. As she was already judging herself in the bathroom mirror at home before leaving, Sophie peeked around the corner to point out that her butt looks like cauliflower. Thanks, kid.

Approaching 35, she wonders if the ponytail and rock-n-roll T-shirt have become a desperate attempt to hold on to what is already gone. It helps to remember that she got cat-called by the construction crew across the street as she unlocked the café this morning. Sure, it was offensive, but that didn't mean it didn't boost her confidence a bit. The memory inspires her to roll her shoulders and flex her arm to tighten the skin that dared mock her. She hears her brain whisper, "Yeah, that vegan tween barely has the energy to lift a muffin. I could definitely take her in a fight."

"Why are you smiling like an executioner?"

Frankie slides two boxes of eggs across the counter. His comment alerts Jules that her thoughts are more easily readable than she believes. She glances again at the girl who never really noticed Jules' existence and shrugs. As she moves the eggs to the back counter, she reads right through Frankie's grim expression. He isn't exactly subtle.

"Goddamn it," she grumbles to herself as she pours him a cup of coffee. A real cup. Like a 1950s diner cup of coffee. With full-fat cream and white sugar.

"What?" he asks as she slides the mug toward him, splashing a bit of hot sin on his fingers.

She raises her eyebrows like a question mark, and he looks away.

"The house is for sale." He says it like it's her fault, and she concentrates on cleaning the espresso machine to keep herself from wrapping the towel around Frankie's neck.

"Please stop driving by," she says, knowing he won't.

"Did you know?"

She responds by changing the subject. "Please tell me you're staying."

He's not letting go. "Did. You. Know?"

She concedes with a shrug and puts her attention on moving the eggs again.

"Why didn't you tell me?"

A million reasons come to her mind, but she settles on one of the kinder options. "I was hoping it wouldn't matter."

He accepts this answer with a shrug and sips his coffee. "Me, too."

"Many people know you. Some even like you. And Shithead's shittiness isn't a secret. So, yes, I was told Shane was selling his house."

"Our house."

With customers within earshot, she figures it is best to change the subject before she lays a line of curse words on the counter. "So, are you staying today?"

"I can't. I have to work."

Goddamn him. "Yes, you do. You have to work *here*. This is your café, remember?"

She watches him look around at the room he built. She knows he misses it and hates him for choosing misery over moving on. It's his process. She's well acquainted with how he operates, but she wouldn't mind if he changed it up this time or, at least, sped it up.

Six years ago, the insurance company where Frankie worked was bought out, and they gave him the option of moving to Tulsa or taking severance. He took the money and opened this coffee shop. For an introvert who had never waited tables, the choice surprised everyone other than Jules. A year before he pulled the trigger on the idea, they had been in a coffee shop that was getting nearly everything wrong. The options. The service. The decor. Frankie gave Jules a detailed breakdown of what he would do differently if he owned it. When he pulled out his phone to show her a Pinterest page dedicated to coffee shops and menu items, she figured it was just a matter of time before it happened. He wanted it to be organic and vegetarian, even though they're a family of carnivores.

It was Jules who drove the unemployed Frankie by the empty garage for sale in Des Moines' warehouse district. The area was quickly becoming a hotbed of downtown renovation. The city razed the formerly dilapidated buildings and made a park behind the building. Across the street, the rubble of a former porn shop set the stage for a future green space in front of the new library.

She suggested he turn his Pinterest page into a reality, and he laughed her off. "Where? In this old garage? What would I call it—*Fuel Injector?*"

The minute he said it aloud, she knew he would make it happen. Jules liked to fantasize, but Frankie didn't daydream; he planned. He was the most fearless, insecure person she'd ever met. Frankie believes he's a passive participant in his life, but she knows he lives with intention. Brooding over Shane is a legitimate devastation, but Jules knows her brother too well. It won't destroy him. She's had 34 years of experience watching him control the perception of his life.

His "I have to go" suggested at least part of him wanted to stay. That was a step forward.

"Fine. Go," she says dramatically before adding, "Damon is grilling tonight if you want to come over. I'm sure Sophie would like to see you."

Frankie shakes his head at her, knowing the spike she's setting up. "If I tell you I'm busy, will you give me shitty uncle guilt?"

Jules can barely fight the smile on her lips. "No, I'm sure she'll understand. I mean, she's seven and you're her favorite uncle, but ..."

Frankie fights his creeping smile. "I'm her only uncle."

"Oh, you're right. So, you ignoring her must *really* sting."

He gulps the last of his coffee and laughs. "You're a bitch."

Fluttering her eyelashes, she adds, "Bring wine."

He slides the coffee mug back to her. When she reaches for it, he pulls it back so they are both holding it. His mood has swung back to the dark side, and she knows why.

"Dad thinks she's coming back on Sunday."

She taps his finger with her own like the smallest of hugs. "I know."

Frankie bites his lip. Searching for words, Jules feels tears form in her eyes just as she watches them build in her brother's. "It's gonna be bad."

She nods. "I know."

He upends their precious moment with a smirk. "Did you hear Joshua Myles was in town?"

She snort-grunt-laughs in a way that draws the attention of everyone in the café. Even the tweens pause their cyber-lives and stare at Jules like they'd forgotten what real people look like. Jules blushes like a porn star in confession as she remembers being touched by someone she keeps telling herself to forget. It was a thousand years and 12 lifetimes ago. Frankie knows and shows no mercy.

"Did you hear me? Joshua Myles is in town."

The joyful sadism on his face is something Jules has missed. But now that it's back, she wishes he'd point it somewhere else. She can't ignore the way hearing Joshua's name spills open the box of Polaroid memories and journal entries from the dusty corners of her mind. Jules realizes she has been holding her breath, hoping it will suffocate the reminiscences. It doesn't work.

"Screw the wine. Bring whiskey."

4

FOLDING.

IT TOOK A LONG TIME for Frankie to love Des Moines. The Midwest can be cruel to a gay boy, especially a creative, shy one. Following a half-assed suicide attempt with fish oil supplements at 17, Frankie plunged into soul-searching and court-ordered therapy. He realized the low-brow bullying and dismissive cruelty was part of his self-discovery and self-acceptance.

This might be a better selling point if he wasn't an almost 40-year-old single gay man living with his dad and driving a minivan that smells like pig shit when you turn on the air conditioner.

Frankie knows he could rearrange the pieces of his life into something more respectable, but he needs the mess right now. He needs the rage and sadness because they're justifiable, given his recent life circumstances. It's harder to explain the same feelings in a better existence. Clinical depression isn't easy in a world that reminds you that "it could always be worse." He doesn't understand why people treat depression like a competition. It's not a matter of sadness looking for justification. It doesn't always feel like misery, though that defines certain moments. It's not a sense of doom, pessimism, or hatred—self-pointing or otherwise—only a life painted in monochromatic shades of melancholy.

Attempts with various medications didn't work. He wasn't seeking numbness, only a bottom that didn't feel bottomless. If your feet can't find the ground, you have nothing to push up from. He has learned to live with this dichotomy. He continues to experience profound joy and happiness, even though he senses a shadow on everything.

So, when the collapse of several parts of his life happened all at once seven months ago, he got to share what he was already feeling in a way that people understood. They could now understand the rain clouds he carried in his pockets as if they had just shown up instead of being there all along.

But he knows that understanding is shutting down. We are a "what doesn't kill you makes you stronger" world. Get up. Dust off. Back to work. Back to living.

Jules has done that. Frankie hasn't seen Jules get emotional about their mother leaving. They searched for the letter she'd left a few times when their father was away. Maybe they could decipher something in it he couldn't. Maybe they would better understand why Clayton believed she was returning on Sunday beyond that it was their 40th wedding anniversary.

"Of course, she'll be here," Clayton had insisted when Frankie and Jules had expressed doubt. He hadn't mentioned it much in the last couple of months, and Frankie had hoped that perhaps his father was making peace with the fact that she's gone. But apparently not.

Frankie clicks on the van's air conditioning, even though he's only a few minutes from work. As the forced air hits his face, he is immediately reminded of the day three years ago when he and Shane discovered their minivan smelled like pig shit. They'd had the van only a few weeks when they were driving back from Clayton's house with Shane's kids in the backseat and clicked on the air. Then-five-year-old Toby was the first to notice it. "What's that smell?"

Frankie and Shane knew it was a farm smell, but Shane couldn't help but add to the teasing, glancing back at Brady. "No more hot dogs for you, I guess."

Brady, all of seven at the time and 50 pounds of raw emotions, burst into tears. "I didn't do it! Toby did! You smelt it; you dealt it! Don't blame me for your poopy pants!"

Toby plugged his nose and pointed at Brady. "Duuuuuuude. Your butt hates you."

Frankie had to stifle his laughter by covering his mouth and directing his attention outside. In the backseat, Brady screamed in tears and reached over to tear Toby apart, his little brother's life only saved by the restraints of Brady's seat belt. "Shut up! Your butt stinks! You did it!"

Back in parent mode, Frankie turned to the boys. "No one pooped their pants. The smell is coming from the farm. That's pig poop you smell. Relax. It will clear away soon."

But it didn't. It lingered for far too long.

"Maybe we ran over some pig shit?" Shane guessed once they were back in town, and the smell hadn't dissipated.

Brady, a stickler for the rules, piped up. "Ouph. Bad word.

Dollar in the jar."

Toby, always a firecracker, had to add. "Maybe Brady fell into the pig shit."

And the screaming and crying and swinging started again. Frankie and Shane failed to remain the mature ones as they giggled through the reprimands.

When they stopped for gas and ice cream, they found the outside air was clear, so they drove the rest of the way home with the windows open, hoping it would air out. It seemed to work until later, when they took the boys back to Shane's ex-wife's house. The air changed odor as soon as they clicked on the air conditioning again.

"Well, crap," Shane had laughed as they figured out the culprit.

"I think you mean 'pig crap,' " Brady said, making himself cackle. He loved to beat Toby to a joke.

After dropping the boys off, Frankie and Shane ran the van through a car wash. Twice. They took it for a deep clean. They had all the filters changed. But, alas, they had to make peace with the poop.

Frankie is laughing at this memory as he pulls into the parking lot at Murray's Industrial. He knows he should hate working here, but he doesn't. After running the cafe for six years and enjoying the gay social scene with Shane, he embraced the break from it all.

He walks through the front door and nods to the receptionist, Gloria, who is busy arguing with someone on the phone. "Like I said, a quarter-inch and a fourth of an inch are the same thing." And then, after a pause, "Sure, hold on, and I'll get a man on the line."

She rolls her eyes and tosses Frankie a smile as she buzzes him through to the warehouse. He hasn't requested a pass card yet because they aren't available to temporary employees. While he's not sure he will ever leave, he also enjoys holding onto the "temporary" title.

Forklifts honk and screech, echoing through the vast warehouse as gruff men with clipboards scream out orders to gruffier men with hard hats. Some nod to Frankie. He hastily waves back as he slips from the warehouse into the quiet file room sanctuary. Windows surround it on two sides and a lot of the warehouse noise still comes through, but in here he's separated from it, like he's underwater. There's more dust than files and the files are not scarce. The company's septuagenarian owner has long refused to trust computers, but he's been convinced by his new, much younger wife to digitize the files. He's agreed, but wants hard copies, "just in case." It's Frankie's job to make sense of the stacks standing waist-high and running the length of one wall as they prepare to scan everything, and the stacks grow daily.

Like now, when his supervisor, Bobby Langston, brings in the order files from the overnight shift. Bobby has made him nervous lately, and he's not sure why, so he tries to keep his distance. He's a beige-on-beige boss whose entire personality seems to hover around the same color palette, so there's nothing to fear. Despite that, he makes Frankie uncomfortable.

Most days, Bobby quickly drops off the files and heads back to the warehouse, but today, he attempts conversation. "Morning, Frankie."

Frankie gives a forced smile that even tastes bad. He isn't

sure how to correct it, so he takes the files from Bobby and walks them to the farthest stack, even though there is no real order to them.

"Morning," Frankie says when he's reached a comfortable distance. "Is it still okay if I leave early today? I wanna help my dad."

Bobby nods, "Of course." After a beat of looking around like he's seeing the file room for the first time, he adds, "How's everything going?"

Frankie senses an attempt to invade his personal space but returns it to the safety of the professional space. "It's fine. It feels like I'm barely making a dent, but the cabinets are filling up, so I guess I am."

Bobby smiles without looking at Frankie and clears his throat. "No, how are things going?"

Sensing the impossibility of redirecting the conversation, Frankie looks down at the manila folder in his hand. He wonders if he could fold himself up and disappear into one of the dusty files. "Things are okay. Thank you for asking."

They've discussed none of the reasons that brought Frankie in to interview for an entry-level job six months ago. When asked why he wanted it, he explained he could use a few months of something quiet. No one mentioned Fuel Injector, even though it was on top of his resume, and Bobby had a Fuel Injector mug on his desk. He was pretty sure that everyone he came across knew what happened with Shane.

Bobby looks like he wants to say more but heads for the door instead. Just as he reaches for the handle, he turns around. "Gloria and I are going to High Life for lunch if you'd like to join us."

They've already had more of a conversation than they've had in six months, and now a lunch invitation? What the hell? "Oh, uh, thanks, but I'm … well, I'm leaving early … so …"

Frankie senses Bobby finds the exchange amusing, and it pisses him off, so he slides on his headphones and disappears down the row of files. Feeling he needs to apologize, he clicks off his music and turns back, but Bobby is gone, and the room is screaming with silence.

5

RORSCHACH.

CLAYTON SPLASHES A BIT of sink water on his face as he washes the tomatoes. They've stopped working in the garden to make lunch, and the day's heat is already getting too much. Every year at this time, he claims it's his last year, that he's giving up, selling the farm, moving to a condo with central air and bingo night. And every year, he means it. At least, he thinks he does. But maybe this year, he actually does. It would make sense, given the year he's had. And when Carol gets back, perhaps it's exactly the kind of new adventure she needs. He imagines them sitting on a small balcony of a condo near downtown, maybe the same building where a couple of friends moved. The place is small and smartly furnished and they are having a summer cocktail from a recipe Carol found in a magazine while she reads through a list of ideas to do with all their newly discovered free time. He will curl his lip at all the suggestions but happily tag along when one of them grabs her interest.

Matches interrupts his daydream as she saddles up beside him in the kitchen with a bowl of lettuce she sets out to rinse off and tear up. "You and Frankie wanna come over later? We're teaching JP how to play cribbage."

Clayton smiles at the mention of the card game, remembering all the nights he and Matches had played with their own grandparents. "You gonna let him win like grandpa let you?"

Matches huffs her indignation. "Let me? You can't let someone win in cribbage. You either win or you don't."

"He wasn't cutthroat with you like he was with me. He never stole pegs from you."

She laughs and nudges him. "Maybe he couldn't because I never gave him anything to steal."

"You wish." He throws a small tomato at her, and it lands in her lettuce bowl. She fishes it out and pops it in her mouth. "Come over. See if you can steal from me if you think you're so good."

"Can't tonight. Jules called. Apparently, Damon is attempting to grill, which means I should fill up on lunch."

They laugh together, knowing Damon is as bad at cooking as he is good at being a husband and father. Most evenings that start with him at the grill end with a brick of charcoal next to a plate of edible sides. One evening even ended with a visit to the ER. Jules is in charge of the side dishes to ensure something remains palatable. She's a good wife to let him continue trying, but everyone secretly hopes she'll soon take the tongs and lighter fluid away from him.

"Frankie going, too?" Matches and Clayton switch places so she can rinse the lettuce, and he can slice the tomatoes.

He nods as he lines up the plump red victims under his butcher knife.

"Good," she says, reminding Clayton that he's not the only one watching his fragile children try to make their way through the winds of change.

"Weird, isn't it? The way life spins in unexpected ways," Matches says as she looks out the window. Clayton follows her eyes to see Pete and JP dragging a plastic bin of potatoes toward the greenhouse. The love in her eyes hits Pete like a laser, and he pauses to trace the energy in the air until he spots her in the window and gives a little wave.

She sighs as she turns back to shake the water off the lettuce. "I was sure Dale was going to be the end of my story. He was supposed to be. He promised me he would be. And then he died, and Pete was there to take me by surprise. To make me remember what living felt like."

Clayton concentrates on the tomatoes, slicing each into perfect, uniform width. He knows his sister is hinting at things she won't actually say, and he opens his mouth to shut her down, but she continues. "And then JP came to stay with us, and an even more unexpected chapter started. I assumed since I never had children that 'grandma' was something I'd never hear. Being a great aunt to Sophie and Frankie's boys—when they were Frankie's boys—was plenty. But now I'm a newlywed and a grandmother. I feel too old to be one and too young to be the other."

Clayton is relieved that the conversation has stayed on her side of the room. "I don't care how young you feel. You seem happy. That's all that matters to me."

She turns to Clayton. "It's not *all* that matters to you.

I wish…"

He looks into her eyes and assumes this will be the conversation he is dreading. He sets the knife down, just to be safe, and she huffs a small laugh.

"I wish you knew … or could see …"

It wasn't like her to struggle for words, so he knew this wasn't easy for her. He also knew he wasn't going to help her question him.

"What, Margaret Ann? What do you wish I could see?" His tone underlined his choice to use her Christian name.

Her eyebrows acknowledged the warning, even if her lips ignored it.

"Your life is on hold. Hers is not."

He felt his teeth grind as he considered a response that didn't taste like spit.

"I know who she is."

"What you want to believe is not the same thing as what, at least part of you, has to know."

"And what is that?" he asks, daring her to say to his face what everyone has certainly been whispering behind his back.

She briefly looks frail as she tries to find the words, and it surprises him enough that he takes a step back and then rests a hand on the fist she has clenching the lettuce. He massages her wrist to loosen her grip, and she swats his hand away, turning to hide the tears in her eyes.

She clears her throat and turns back to him, her composure restored. "Do you have any bacon or are these going to be lettuce and tomato sandwiches?"

He considers taking the conversation back to where it

was headed. It hadn't occurred to him that maybe he did want to talk about it, fight about it, hash it out. He suddenly has things to say, but they are interrupted when JP clears his throat in the doorway.

"Uh, Mr. Parker? Do the horses get lunch, too?"

Clayton considers whether he should stay in the conversation with Matches or return to the tasks at hand. One is probably more necessary, but the other is easier. "Well, I guess they need something. Are you offering to help?"

Watching a kid too cool to be impressed try to suppress joy is always a pleasure, and JP's epic failure at apathy is a sight to behold. "Sure. Whatever."

He slips back outside to wait. Clayton slides the plate of tomatoes to Matches. She wipes her hands with a kitchen towel. "Thank you for appeasing him. I think he almost smiled."

"Oh, he's a good kid. Being a teenager ain't his fault. The bacon is—"

She swats him away. "I always know where the bacon is."

He taps her on the nose, something he knows she hates, and she growls her disdain while wiping away the itch as a smile teases the corner of her mouth.

With something resembling peace between them, Clayton goes outside and finds JP trying to balance on one of the wobbly rocks surrounding the rose garden. "Careful now. Frankie fell on the roses, trying that same stunt. More than once. You might smell good, but you'll be scratched up and bloody for sure. Not exactly a winning combination for your lady friends."

JP blushes and hops off the rock to tag along behind

Clayton. "I don't have any lady friends."

"Boyfriend?"

This question seems to stun the boy faster than a rock to the head. "What?! Nooooo."

Clayton laughs as they enter the barn. "Okay. Calm down. It's just a question. I don't care either way, just in case."

"I'm not gay," JP says in a way that sounds like all the times Frankie said the same thing. This time, however, Clayton actually believes JP.

He drags a bucket of old vegetables out from under a broken workbench and pushes it with his foot toward JP. The kid picks up the bucket and waddles it to the fence, where Rorschach, an American paint horse, happily greets him with a swish of his tail. JP glances back at Clayton for direction.

"He'll eat off your hand but won't bite you. It's okay."

JP's lip curls down with uncertainty, but he grabs a handful of carrots and carefully extends them to the horse, who quickly snatches them up. JP laughs out loud but then swallows his excitement as he looks back at Clayton, fearing his happiness may have been discovered.

Clayton joins him at the gate just as Tie Dye, Rorschach's sister, trots over to make sure she gets some lunch as well. Clayton brushes her blond mane off her eyes and feeds her a carrot, glancing over at JP's wide-eyed wonderment at these gorgeous creatures. "Thanks for helping out today. I'm sure you'd rather be doing something else with your summer."

JP shakes his head, handing Rorschach a head of cabbage. "Nah, this is way cooler than being with my other grandparents. They only have a dumb cat that doesn't even like string."

This makes Clayton laugh as he gives Tie Dye a beet. "Well, that's good; I thought this might be pretty boring for a city kid like you."

JP picks up a horse brush and looks at Clayton for permission. Clayton responds by lifting the rope off the gate and letting it drift open. JP carefully approaches Rorschach, who seems hopeful that the brush is a potato. Discovering it is not, he wheezes in disappointment and turns his attention to the hay on the ground.

"Chicago is loud. I didn't realize that the country could be loud, too, but it's a way different kind of noise. I like it. Except the coyotes. That's just weird."

Clayton watches the boy for a moment before treading into delicate territory. "When are your parents coming back?"

JP pauses slightly from his brushing but then goes right back to it with vigor. "Well, my dad is supposed to be home by September, but it will probably get extended. Mom was transferred to Iraq, probably until Christmas. She says she'll be back this year, but she said that last year."

Clayton uses his hands to brush Tie Dye down when he senses her jealousy over her brother getting groomed. "You've got good parents. Brave people. I know that doesn't make it easy for them to be away, but they are doing the most challenging of work."

"I know," JP says. He pauses his brushing duties and glances over at Clayton. "Can I ask you something that I'm not supposed to ask you?"

Clayton smiles at the sweet kid. "I asked you if you were gay, so I think you're entitled to any question you might have."

JP blushes and nods. "Right on."

He goes back to brushing, apparently needing to be distracted from his own question. "Where's Mrs. Parker?"

It wasn't the question Clayton was expecting. In some ways, it was, but he expected to be asked when Carol was coming back. For some reason, it's startling to be asked where she is because Clayton suddenly becomes shockingly aware that he doesn't actually know. While he might imagine or guess, he can't answer with any certainty. It takes a moment for him to find his footing in the question, and he studies the eyes of Rorschach, wondering if the old boy knows something he doesn't. Carol loved these horses and spent hours out here with them. They probably carry at least a few secrets she whispered into their coats.

He turns to catch JP glancing away, probably confused by the way Clayton was standing still and staring at the horse.

"Mrs. Parker needed a vacation, so she went away for a bit, but she's coming back on Sunday. It's our 40th anniversary. She'll be here. I'm sorry if anyone made you feel like you shouldn't ask me that."

JP sets the brush down and wipes his hands off on his jeans. "I hope she comes back."

Clayton puts his arm around the kid to lead him back toward the house when they hear Matches holler that lunch is ready.

"I know she will."

6

BONES.

OTHER THAN OPEN MIC nights, Jules's favorite time in Fuel Injector is the quiet after the morning rush. Her day starts when her nights used to end, back when she was wild and free. Now, she's elbow-deep in coffee grounds and caffeine zombies before the sun has cracked the horizon. But around 10 a.m., it all gets quiet. This city runs on a nine-to-five schedule, and most people spend their days tucked in some variation of a cubicle. During the week, the café gets peaceful, sometimes even empty between breakfast and lunch.

This is when Jules actually wakes up. She stands outside for a moment once things slow down and breathes in the smell of the day. Even when it's raining. Even when the temperature has to reach up to find zero. With her lungs full and her head cleared, she tucks herself into the small office behind the kitchen area and does the bookkeeping. She acts like she hates it, but she secretly loves it. She wasn't a great math student—hell, she wasn't a great student, period—and the spreadsheets filled her with blind terror when she first started. But then she found the patterns, understood the magic, the rhythm in the pluses and minuses, and it filled her with calm. At least something made sense.

She was finishing the inventory report when Varina, the barista most likely to get fired, pushed back the curtain.

"Watch the counter for a sec, wouldja?"

Varina often forgets she's the employee, not the boss. Jules stares at her for a moment, waiting for the "please" she knows isn't coming. Instead, Varina yawns with a stretch that turns her tank top into a halter top, showing off the disconnected collection of tattoos on her midsection. Jules sets down her pen and stands, hoping Varina is done talking. But she's not.

"By the way, organic tampons are bullshit. I feel like there's bark in my beaver teeth."

Varina scratches her nether region and walks away, leaving Jules trying to remove the vivid image from her mind as she heads out front. She finds a man in a cowboy hat standing with his back to the counter, facing the downtown skyline through the front windows. He must be from out of town, she thinks. No one local takes time to look at the city.

"Hi there."

He turns back to her with a smile that apparently makes a person want to slap someone because that's exactly what she does. She reaches across the counter and smacks his face, sending his hat sailing across the café.

"Joshua Myles! You dirty bitch! What are you doing here?!"

She doesn't even bother to go around the counter, instead

crawling over it to hug him. They spin in an unbalanced embrace for a moment, laughing and talking at the same time.

"What are you doing here?"

"Where's your brother?"

"You look great, Jules. Or is it Julie now?"

They laugh at the madness of the moment and take a beat to calm themselves as Joshua retrieves his hat from under one of the tables. Unable to stop herself, she pulls him into a hug when he turns back to her as unexpected tears spill down her face. Joshua Myles. A man from her past. A body that knew her body before she became who she is. Before he became who he is.

Back when they were high school sweethearts about to graduate, he told her he was moving to Nashville to pursue his music. The work has been paying off as his star is currently on the rise, with a string of songs starting to climb the country charts. She pulls herself together, focusing on straightening his hat and smoothing out his shirt, careful to avoid too much eye contact for fear it could lead someplace dangerous. "I'd apologize, but you're a superstar now. I'm sure you get greetings like that all the time."

" 'Superstar' might be a stretch, but I like that you think it might be true."

Jules laughs. Her whole body feels electric, and she tries to shake it off. "Shut up. You don't have to downplay it for me just because I told you it would probably never happen."

"Damn, I had no intention of reminding you that you said that, but since you brought it up … I told you so."

She steps toward him but then steps back. "Slick. Using

one of your own song titles to remind me what I got so very wrong. Good on you, Mr. Myles. Seriously though, why are you in town? I thought you'd never be back here."

"I'm out at SoundFarm. I'm working on a couple of songs for my next album. Someone mentioned you were working here. I couldn't be close and not see you."

She can feel him looking at her, knowing her, smirking at the way she obviously avoids looking at his face, his eyes, his lips.

He steps forward, and she's both grateful and terrified to find the counter directly behind her. He puts his hands out on the counter, trapping her between the arms she used to know so very well. She braces herself for impact and looks up at him. "Well, thank you, Mr. Fancypants, for throwing a bone to us little people."

He raises an eyebrow, and it feels like an ice cube is being slid up her inner thigh. She is determined to remain cool but can feel her knees shaking. She holds her breath when he leans forward and whispers, "Once upon a time, you mighta been looking to catch that bone."

It's ridiculous enough to break the spell, and her release comes out in a cackle as she pushes him away. "You better write that one down before you forget it. I expect to hear it on the radio within the year."

Before any more lines get crossed, Varina walks in. "Holy country biscuits in my britches! You are Joshua Freakin' Myles!"

Joshua pulls his attention away from Jules as Varina races behind the counter, looking for something Jules rightfully assumes is her phone when she uncovers it from behind the bakery case. Joshua extends a hand to her over the counter.

"Howdy. It's always nice to meet a fan."

She snorts a laugh as she struggles to figure out her phone.

"Oh my God, no, no, no! I am not a fan at all. What am I, 50? Too much twang and cheap beer for me. But I have friends that would swallow their own faces if they knew I was standing next to you right now. Well, mostly my mother's friends, but still … Can I get a picture?"

Jules laughs at Joshua's confusion over this crass girl. Varina comes around the counter and hands her phone to Jules. "Take our picture."

Varina fluffs her hair and adjusts her breasts before directing Joshua to put his arm around her, which he does in stunned silence. Varina leans against his chest and puts her hand on his stomach, just above his belt buckle, making him gasp. Jules snaps the picture, savoring Joshua's expression. She quickly texts the photo to herself and hands Varina her phone.

"We're going for a walk. Can you prep for lunch?"

Varina huffs. "By myself?"

Jules takes Joshua's hand and leads him out. "It's bread, Varina. Figure it out."

On the sidewalk, Jules drops the hand of a still traumatized Joshua. He looks from her back to the door of the café. "I think I hate her."

"You're not alone."

He shakes his head and reaches to wrap his arm around her, but she steps out of reach, leading him down the sidewalk. "How long are you in town?"

"Just until Monday."

"That's good and bad news, I guess." She runs her fingers through her hair, finding the bread tie holding back her bangs. She untwists it, using her fingers to shake out her hair.

"Why is it good news that I'm leaving on Monday?"

"That's not what I meant." It was what she meant, and they both knew why.

"How's your family?" she asks.

He grabs her arm, stopping her. "Can we stop for a minute?"

She realizes she's winded, almost running away from him and everything he's making her feel. She nods and leads him to a bench on the edge of the sculpture park that took over an old city block.

They settle down, and she suddenly feels exhausted. She looks down at her hands and can't help glancing over at his thighs, the muscles thick under his jeans. She remembers all the times she'd lay in his lap, his fingers playing with her hair as they talked and dreamed and loved. They were such children then, desperate to be grown up. What she wouldn't give to be back there again. Innocent and full of promise and swagger.

He brings her attention back to the present. "To answer your question, my family is fine. More importantly, how are you?"

She notices a bare thread in the hem of his jeans near his knee, and she wonders how much would unravel if she reached over and gave it a tug. "We're surviving," she says, looking over at one of the prominent statues in the park, a person sitting with their hands on their knees completely constructed from steel alphabet letters. It suddenly makes sense to her how a person could be built from hidden words.

"How much of what I've heard is true?" Joshua asks.

She sighs and turns back to him. "Well, seven months ago, my mother walked out without warning. She left a letter that only my father has read. Two days later, Frankie caught Shane in bed with someone else."

He lets out a low whistle. "Yep, pretty much what I've heard. I thought your parents were so in love. No one looked at a woman like your father looked at your mother."

"My dad actually seems to be doing better than Frankie somehow. Frankie is a mess. He quit the café. He quit hosting and performing at open mic night. He quit … life. My dad, though, seems fine. Delusion will do that, I guess. He's convinced she's coming back on Sunday."

"Their anniversary?"

Her eyes shoot to him. "How do you know it's their anniversary?"

He tips his head and squints in the sun as he looks at her. "I remember. July 25th. Christmas in July."

She rolls her eyes. "It's ridiculous. We haven't done any decorating or even talked about it. It was always something that my mom commandeered."

They sit silently for a minute, and then he nudges her with his shoulder. "For the record, I asked you how you were doing, and you told me how everyone else was doing but you."

She lets out a long, low breath. "I'm not even sure. The numbness is my armor, I guess. My dad got knocked down and then Frankie got sucker punched, and I stood on the side, watching the crash and burn."

"But you weren't on the sidelines. Your mom left you, too."

"I know, but I get an escape from it. I'm there for my dad and brother when they need me, but then I get to go home to my own family."

"So, all the rumors I heard are true," he says, reaching over to tap her wedding ring. She lifts her hand to wave it at him.

"Yes. Mrs. Damon Farris. Mother of the illustrious Sophie Clayton Farris, queen of the universe."

She opens the locket around her neck to show a small photo of her daughter. Joshua leans close to look at it, close enough that his hair brushes Jules' lips. He looks up at her and sits back, sensing the way she's tense from his proximity.

"You do know that when Chrissy told me you were married, she had to whisper that your husband is Black or, as she enunciated, 'Af-ri-can-A-mer-i-can,'" They laugh. Joshua's sister has always insisted she's open-minded and liberal but has failed every test to prove it.

"I'm sure," Jules says. "Watching her find out Frankie was gay is one of the greatest 30-second silent horror films I've ever seen."

They laugh again. "I should get back. There's a good possibility Varina has set the place on fire, and we don't even have a grill."

Joshua stands and pulls her up beside him. "Gotta say, Jules, I never thought you'd be the settling kind."

She leads him back toward the café. "I left for a while. Albuquerque. Austin. Portland. Then, one day, I realized the thing I wanted, I'd left behind."

She hopes he doesn't say what she has invited him to say, but he just can't help blowing a kiss against the walls of her comfort zone. "I feel like that sometimes."

She tries to ignore all that could mean, even though it's impossible to deny that the space between them isn't melting away.

7

LIGHTS.

IN THE OLD DAYS, finding a string of holiday lights at a hardware store didn't require a map, and the store with the string of lights didn't also sell snorkeling gear, coyote urine, and a sandcastle Bundt cake pan. Clayton regrets shrugging off the offer for guidance from the three employees he passed in the first 30 seconds of entering Menards, the closest home improvement store to the farm. He could certainly find string lights without help. He was certainly wrong.

All those helpful smiles seem to have vanished. There's not an employee to be found, just other customers wandering aimlessly from aisle to aisle, finding more things they don't need than they do. He passes a particularly frazzled-looking man trailing behind a wife, seemingly on a mission to find at least one thing in every row to add to their cart. The man's smile to Clayton feels like a distress call, so he obliges with a question.

"I don't suppose you've seen string lights anywhere?" he asks the man.

The wife speaks for them both. "We haven't, but that reminds me …"

She doesn't finish her thought, instead nearly pulling her husband off-balance as she leads the cart around the corner.

Clayton starts to follow them, thinking maybe his question had inspired the woman to head in a direction that would somehow feed his quest as well, but he stops when he finds himself in a maze of patio furniture and grills. He'd wanted a new grill for a while since the one at home lacked all the bells and whistles that now seemed to be standard. Carol had insisted the one they had was fine, ignoring his protests that it didn't have a rib rack stand, pizza stone insert, or smoker.

He is drawn to a display of grill guns whose use seems both mysterious and necessary but is distracted by a woman bent over a large box, trying to hoist it onto a dolly that keeps rolling away from her. He hears her curse under her breath as she tries to keep the dolly in place with one foot while lugging the box toward it, trying to shimmy it into place.

"Can I help you?" he asks, placing his hand on the dolly's handle without waiting for an answer.

The woman turns to thank him when she recognizes Clayton. "Well, hello you!" Her smile threatens to split her face, and Clayton steps back from her exuberance.

Mona Fontaine has the name and attitude of a drag queen, but she is not one. She's a firecracker in her 60s, whom Clayton has known for years. Her son, Joey, and Jules had been classmates since at least junior high, perhaps even longer. Joey owned a gay bar in town, but he died a couple of years ago, and Mona had taken it over. Clayton and Carol had been in a couple of times to see her, but Clayton eventually clued into some unspoken tension between the women. Clayton had asked Carol about it, but the response was little more than a brittle, "She's fine." So, he gave up suggesting that they stop in after the third time Carol found an excuse not to.

"Thank God you came along," Mona says, reaching over to pat him on the arm. "Looking for customer service in this place is like looking for nipples in a bag of dicks."

Her bawdiness had always made Clayton slightly uncomfortable, but there was something delightful about her as well. He can only nod and lift the box onto the dolly. As he does, he notices that it's the grill he daydreamed about. He hears the entire ad play in his head. *The GrillMaster Elite 9000 redefines outdoor luxury with its sleek, brushed stainless steel finish and polished gunmetal accents. Equipped with multiple burners, built-in rotisserie, infrared searing, and Wi-Fi connectivity, it offers unparalleled precision and convenience. The soft blue LED display and integrated lighting enhance its modern aesthetic, making it more than just a grill—it's a state-of-the-art outdoor kitchen.*

"Nice choice," he says as he runs his hand over the box like it's the body of a sleek classic car.

"It's too much for the bar, but I can't help overindulging those queens," she tells him. "We've been doing hot dogs and stuff on Sunday afternoons. One of the dumbass employees didn't bring our old grill inside last weekend, and it was stolen. So, here I am."

She sighs and pushes the dolly down the aisle where they meet an overly friendly employee who looks at them like he's discovered them hiding in the store after hours instead of in the middle of the day. "Can I help you with anything?"

Clayton can see that Mona is considering sharing her honest opinion and cuts her off at the pass. "I'm looking for Christmas lights."

The man's smile melts against his teeth. "It's July."

"We didn't ask for a calendar, dear. We asked for Christmas lights. If that's too confusing, perhaps saying 'string lights' is easier," Mona responds, and Clayton blushes at both her brusqueness and the "we" in her response. He glances down the aisle, expecting to find Carol with her arms crossed while she snips, "She's fine."

The employee straightens his name tag and rubs away a smudge that has changed "Chad" to "Chat." "There might be some in aisle 14 with the leftover July Fourth stuff, but I'm not sure."

"Thanks, honey," Mona says with all the sincerity of a backhand. "You've been an epic help."

Chad forces himself to light up his smile again, but his eyes remain dead as he walks away, leaving Mona shaking her head. "I swear, the older I get, the fewer people I like."

She uses the dolly to move Clayton along, nearly scooping him up onto the grill box. As they meander toward aisle 14, their conversation drifts through the familiar cadence of Midwestern small talk. They swap predictions about the August heat wave, wondering if it'll scorch the crops or bring a surprise thunderstorm to cool things down. The state fair, just weeks away, takes center stage as they debate which food-on-a-stick will be this year's favorite and what will be carved out of butter. They share their latest roadside sweet corn finds, each claiming to have discovered the best vendor: Clayton's is Morton Jeffries' peaches and cream corn just off Highway 30, while Mona prefers the butter and sugar corn sold by the Hollister girls from the retired purple pickup collecting dust near the old red barn out by the Milo silo.

By the time they find the lights they are looking for, Clayton has all but forgotten what brought him here. He can't remember the last time he was part of a conversation that wasn't tinged with questions about Carol and his kids. Mona only brought them up in passing, mentioning his family as one of many who used to take part in a now-defunct farm tour that the chamber of commerce was trying to relaunch. It was probably the longest Clayton had gone without Carol being front and center in his mind since the moment he'd picked up her letter.

Now, he's thinking of her again as Mona holds up four boxes of white string lights. Two that blink and two that don't. It's not nearly enough to light the house as they have in the past, and Clayton is torn between whether or not to buy the ones that blink or not.

"I think she likes the twinkles," he says to himself, just as he hears Mona say, "Call me crazy, but I always find the twinkling ones kind of sad. It feels like something is fading away."

Exhausted from the uncertainty, Clayton takes all four boxes from her and drops them on top of the grill box. "Screw it."

Mona laughs softly. "Whoa, tiger. Don't go overboard."

Clayton looks at Mona more closely as she flicks a row of

star-spangled teddy bears in the nose one by one, knocking them onto their backs. Carol was right. She is fine.

They check out together, and when they reach the parking lot, Mona stops in the middle. "Well, shit."

When Clayton asks what's wrong, she points to her old Buick Regal and then back to the enormous box for the grill. It was never going to fit in her car. Though she repeatedly insists it's her stupid mistake to deal with, Clayton insists he can bring the grill by the bar on Saturday after the farmers' market. What's the point of having a pickup if not to rescue moments like this? She eventually relents and insists he come have a drink on the house after the market.

After loading the grill box into his truck, Mona honks and waves, and she drives away. Clayton stares at the box sitting in the bed of his truck for a beat and then makes a decision. First, he goes back inside and buys his own GrillMaster Elite 9000. Then, he drives out to Milo to pick up some of the butter and sugar corn from the Hollister girls to see exactly what Mona was raving about.

8

BURNT.

"OH ... EM ... GOD." Jules has never seen her friend, Heidi, quite so flummoxed and, apparently, it's all Jules's fault. Evidently, Jules failed to mention that she once dated the new country superstar Joshua Myles. This revelation accidentally spills onto the picnic table when Heidi starts gushing that she heard a rumor that he was back in town and that she would simply die if she saw him. Jules confirmed that she had actually seen him earlier that day. She didn't just see him but actually spoke to him. Hugged him, even, because they were friends and had dated in high school. Jules assumed Heidi knew this fact about her past. She clearly did not, as Heidi is now blushing, pale, and tugging on her humidity-suffering, carrot-red curls with one hand while her other hand fans herself with a paper plate. Moments ago, the plate held a pile of potato chips. The chips are now scattered around her, crumb-staining her Sugarland T-shirt.

"How did I not know this?" She is demanding, with an unexpected amount of venom dripping from her horror film smile. "You know more about me than my own husband does, and somehow I didn't know you dated Joshua Myles?" Saying it out loud seems to both exhaust and exhilarate her, and she drops the plate and starts picking at the chips on her chest, popping each into her mouth.

"Seriously," she continues, her tone shifting to titillated curiosity. "You must tell me everything. Every. Last. Detail."

Jules gathers her thoughts as Damon slides open the patio door and comes out, balancing a plate of burgers. She watches him head to the grill where the odds are good that he's about to burn dinner. For some reason, it feels odd to talk about Joshua in front of Damon. It's not like her old boyfriend is a secret; she already told Damon that Joshua surprised her at the café today. But somehow, it feels like she's saying too much. Maybe she's worried that if she talks about him, it will be obvious that his name on her tongue tastes like the most wicked candy—a guilty pleasure she can't quite bring herself to spit out. Every time she mentions Joshua, there's a tingling, an awareness, as if she's inviting him into a space that should belong solely to Damon.

She glances at her husband, grounding herself in the life they've built together. Damon's thick back still carries the confidence of his youth. He's now softened into the comfortable roundness of fatherhood, and he is her rock. His dark skin glows with warmth, and his handsome features reflect the gentleness that only deepens as he looks at her. He is the embodiment of the love and ease they've shared for a decade. But there's no denying that a distance has been growing between them lately. Maybe that's just part of what it means to love someone for a long time. The comfortable familiarity becomes so commonplace that the lack of friction becomes mistaken for distance. As she tries to build a bridge back to Damon in her mind, the memory of Joshua stirs a treacherous thrill that she struggles to push away.

Heidi isn't helping with her eyes begging for all the sordid details.

"It's weird," she says, trying to shrug it off. "I forget that he's that Joshua Myles. To me, he's just some guy I dated in high school. We were young and dumb together."

Her father pipes up from the other end of the table with a laugh. "Just some guy? You kids were crazy about each other. Nearly impossible to keep you two apart."

"Duh," Heidi says. "You've seen him, right? Heard him? Watched that ass swing? It would take a crowbar to pull me away from him, given the chance."

Something occurs to Heidi that makes her eyes go wide. "Wait, did you guys …" She glances at Clayton and turns to Jules as her voice drops an octave and slides into a pornographic whisper. "Do it?"

Jules blushes, which is the only confirmation Heidi needs to squeal with jealous excitement and suck down the rest of her beer in two large gulps. Jules checks to see how much her father has overheard, not that he would be surprised. When she was 16 and heading out for a camping trip with friends that included Joshua, she found a box of condoms tucked in with the trail mix and six-pack of soda her mother packed into the back of Joshua's car. Luckily, Clayton had turned away from Heidi's interrogation and was watching Frankie, who was looking off the deck into the backyard with sadness in his eyes.

Jules follows Frankie's stare to find Sophie, all eight years of 30-pound caramel-colored princess power, warding over Heidi's bigger but intimidated sunburnt sons, Brooks and Sawyer. She guesses that Frankie is missing Shane's kids, the kids that were his, too, for a while. She'd much rather distract her brother than impress Heidi with stories of her high-school crush. But Heidi hasn't had her fill. She slaps Jules's hand.

"More. More. More. Tell me more."

Jules tucks her hair behind her ear and glances at Damon at the grill, the flames already shooting up to his shoulder height, threatening to make her a widow her at any moment. She jumps up and approaches Damon, sliding her arm around his waist, as much to remind herself of the safety she finds against his body as to pull him back from the flames. He turns and gives her a quick kiss on the cheek, and it nearly brings tears to her eyes, the simple gesture bringing her back down to earth.

Heidi is nearly hyperventilating as she tugs on Jules' shirt sleeve. "Teeeeeellllll meeeeeee."

Jules collapses down next to her again after yanking her arm away more aggressively than she intended to. She suddenly feels more annoyed than nostalgic. Of course, she loves Damon and her life. Joshua is past tense.

"There's nothing to tell. Yeah, we dated in high school. He was fun. It's funny that he's a country star now because there's nothing country about the Joshua Myles that I remember. He was a rich city kid. Heck, he didn't even mow his own lawn."

Heidi giggles uncontrollably. "He could mow my lawn." She glances over at Clayton, ready to apologize. But he's still focused on Frankie. She looks back at Jules and mouths, "I'm sorry," while patting her armpits. "Just talking about him is making me sweat."

Jules can only laugh at her. "Are you sure? It's 86 degrees with 90 percent humidity. I'm not sure Joshua Myles is what's making you sweat."

Any filter Heidi once had is gone. "Well, he's certainly making me wet."

She hears herself and gasps, covering her face. Jules doesn't know how to comfort her friend from the horrors of her own pubescence, so she decides to make it worse. "He's only here until Monday, but he's coming back for the state fair. We'll have to go. I could introduce you."

Heidi almost swoons as she processes this new information. Jules savors the moment of power, still surprised that people moon over Joshua like this. Since she's moved him back to the safety of a "used to be," he no longer threatens to topple her sense of balance.

To add fuel to the fire, Frankie finally decides to pipe up. "You should invite him to the open mic tomorrow night."

It's too much for Heidi, and she stands up, pacing back and forth between the table and the grill. Damon pushes her back with the tongs to protect her from the flames. "Oh God, oh God, oh God, oh God. Do you think he'd come?"

Jules glares at Frankie's kerosene grin and tries to comfort Heidi. "Like I said, he's only here until Monday. I'm sure he's busy."

Damon doesn't help when he adds, "You should ask him.

It'd be good buzz for the biz."

Heidi looks like she might actually burst into tears. And then she does exactly that. She actually cries. "Do you think he would? I mean, I could bring my sister. She'd love to meet him. And, ya know, she's finally done with chemo."

Jules can only shake her head. "Seriously? Are you really playing the cancer card?"

Heidi nods unapologetically. "Use what you got."

Jules sighs her surrender. "I'll ask, but it seems weird. And stupid."

The noise that comes out of Heidi is nothing short of primal and the neighbor's dog reacts with a terrified howl. Everyone is staring at her, including the kids who have come to stand at the edge of the deck. Brooks and Sawyer are wide-eyed and holding hands, terrified of this version of their usually placid mother. Sophie stands beside them with a twisted smile, enjoying the titillating chaos.

Heidi recovers and explains, "Weird and stupid is hot!"

Once again, she stands, now fanning herself with her long floral skirt, which unfortunately turns a simple barbecue into a burlesque show. Jules grabs Heidi's skirt and returns it to its proper job as a curtain over Heidi's lady business, though everyone now clearly knows that Heidi is a fan of Wonder Woman briefs.

Heidi is too distracted to care. "Can I tell people about you and Joshua? Wait, is he a secret?"

"No, he's not a secret but—"

Heidi has heard all she needs and darts away—or tries to until she slams into the sliding glass door leading to the kitchen. Everyone gasps, but Heidi turns back with a timid giggle and rubs away the pain as she calmly opens the door and slips inside. A moment later, she is heard screaming into her phone with her sister.

Jules watches Heidi's silhouette flailing about inside until the amusement turns to boredom. She turns back to all the men and Sophie staring at her as if expecting her to make sense of what they've witnessed. She can only shrug.

"The power of celebrity," she says by way of explanation.

"The burgers are done," Damon announces, and everyone winces as he sets the platter on the table. Surprisingly, they look pretty good this time.

"Huh," Clayton proclaims, unable to suppress his surprise that they might actually be edible. Everyone is openly staring at the burgers, unable to trust what they see.

Damon looks at everyone, confused by their reaction, as Heidi continues yelping and yapping inside. "Are you guys gonna eat, or what?"

The kids inch toward the table as if approaching a plate full of Brussels sprouts, but Frankie leans forward and grabs a burger, taking a bite. "Not bad, Damon," he says. "You actually left the charcoal in the grill this time."

Damon snaps the grill tongs at Frankie with a flat "ha ha." As everyone else digs in, Jules pauses to smile at something she hasn't seen in a long time.

Frankie is laughing.

9

WHISKEY.

AFTER DINNER, the conversation hits a lull. When the plates are empty and the bellies are full, Frankie excuses himself to use the bathroom but, really, he needs some time alone, so he hides in the kitchen. He's enjoying himself tonight, but it's hard for him to be here. The wounds of a thousand memories are especially sharp in Jules's house. He and Shane spent so many hours here, watching Shane's kids play with Sophie. He adores his sister, but her contentment now feels vulgar, and he sometimes feels like running his minivan through her living room.

He pushes the hit-and-run fantasy out of his mind and retrieves a bottle of expensive whiskey he hid in the pantry. Like a boozy bloodhound, Jules is right next to him the minute he pops the cap off. "Goddamn you. I knew you brought this."

He opens a cupboard, takes out two SpongeBob sippy cups, and loads them with a healthy pour. "I don't want to share it with Heidi. It's not cheap, but she is."

Jules jabs him with her elbow but doesn't disagree as she takes a sip. Frankie is a more aggressive drinker, at least tonight, and refills his cup almost immediately as he scans the collection of photographs on the refrigerator. He's in a few of them, and he's trying to remember what life felt like back then. In one, he and a very pregnant Jules are laughing hysterically, both on the verge of becoming a blur. In another, he's giving grumpy-faced Sophie a cheeky side-eye from under a crooked Santa hat. Was he really as happy as he looked?

Another photo catches his eye. Jules snatches it from the fridge and wads it up. But she's too late. He's seen enough. "Toby's birthday."

"Do you realize that I was almost a celebrity wife?" she responds in an attempt to change the subject.

Her attempt fails. "I remember that moment clearly. Toby was turning nine. Brady was six. It was my last party with them, and I didn't know it."

Jules looks at him like she might have something poignant to add. But she has nothing. Instead, she says, "The last time I had sex with Joshua, I told him I thought his music was a waste of time."

Frankie doesn't care about her memories; he cares about his own, so he tries to grab the wadded Polaroid out of Jules's hand. She's tougher than she looks and shoves it into the garbage disposal. Before he can interfere, she hits the switch, sending the blades spinning. He jumps back from the violent grinding sound.

"Jesus Christ! What is wrong with you?" he asks, hating that he has to remind himself not to shove his hand into the grinding drain.

The question makes her laugh, and she needs a minute to collect herself. Jules clicks off the disposal and the grinding comes to a halt. Frankie can only stare at the black hole in the drain holding the shreds of his used-to-be.

"Say 'thank you,' Frankie."

He's mocking her before he can stop himself, using the girly voice he used to torture her with when they were kids. "Thank you, Frankie."

Jules rolls her eyes, then pours herself another drink. Part of him wants to apologize, but a bigger part wants to twist the knife. "Did your reunion with Joshua turn R-rated?"

"Don't be an asshole," she says as she takes a sip but then moves the glass out of her reach.

"That's not a 'no,' " he replies, reaching over to slide her cup back in front of her. She can't help herself and takes a sip.

"If it was a 'yes,' you're probably the only person I would tell; I hope you know that."

They hear Clayton laugh outside, and it stops their moment. Frankie leans over the counter to peek outside, seeing their dad laughing at something Sophie is showing him. It brings tears to his eyes to see his father happy, and that makes him feel like shit, so he pours his drink down his throat, hoping it drowns the darkness. He can feel Jules behind him, thinking so loudly that she might as well be shouting.

"What?" he asks, acknowledging how well they can read each other.

She shakes her head and starts to busy herself with imaginary crumbs near the toaster. But then she turns back to him with a burst of a question, probably louder than she intends. "Do you think Mom is happy?"

He answers without thinking. "I don't care."

His coldness stabs her in a way that she actually reaches for her own heart. "Jesus, Frankie …"

He crosses his arms over his chest to keep his insides from bursting out. "I know in my mind that they aren't connected, but my heart blames her for what happened with Shane. If she hadn't left, I wouldn't have been at Dad's, and Shane wouldn't have been with… whoever."

Words are coming out faster than he can stop them, and he's losing the battle to contain his tears. "And if mom hadn't left, maybe I would have been in a different state of mind. I know I shouldn't say that, but I mean it. I wanted to be able to forgive Shane. Maybe it's not even about forgiving him. I miss the boys. My boys, even though they were never really mine. I miss being a dad more than I miss Shane, and it feels like a punch in the gut every time I breathe."

He wipes his eyes, trying to pull the truth out of the air. But he can't. It's out there. It wasn't a secret, but he also hadn't said it out loud.

"And you blame Mom?"

The question pulls out the last peg holding up the floodgates, and he starts to cry harder, sinking into his little sister's arms. "I have to. Hating her helps me handle the pain of missing them."

She rocks him for a minute, and briefly, Frankie feels his mother's arms around him. That is, of course, until Jules speaks. "That's really fucked up."

The sliding glass door opens, letting in a burst of evening

humidity as everyone parades in off the deck, all in the middle of various conversations. Frankie ducks into the small bathroom off the kitchen, listening as leftovers are sorted, stored, or discarded. He hears the kids ask if it's time for ice cream or pie or s'mores or if there's a way to have a little bit of all of them. The sound of family can feel simultaneously like a pull and a push, and Frankie welcomes the chaos. The madness makes sense, to feel so close and so far in a single moment. He leans his head against the cool door, hearing his father rummaging through the pantry in the hallway. If he could reach through the door, he would pull his father into a hug. He couldn't, he shouldn't, he won't—but the possibility lingers as if a hug between this particular father and son wouldn't feel forced in some parallel universe.

He washes his face and looks at himself in the mirror. He is briefly startled by what he sees. He has never had much of a habit of looking in the mirror. He does, of course, know what he looks like, but he rarely really looks at himself. With his short, buzzed hair and scruffy face, it's easy for him to get ready in the morning without glancing at his reflection.

But right now, he's looking. He leans close enough to the mirror that his vision blurs, and then he steps back. That person, the one in the mirror, is a collection of 10,000 experiences that have taken the shape of a body looking for purpose. There are lifetimes living behind the scratches and scars, the wonders and doubts, the what-ifs and the won't-bes. And what do they all mean? Children are given grace for being confused as they search for meaning. But adults are expected to have it figured out. When does a person become who they are? Life happens so gradually that you miss the becoming. One day, you're a kid kicking on a swing, trying to take flight, and the next, you're hiding in your sister's bathroom, leaning against the sink and staring in the mirror with a soft fascination at how mysterious it all seems.

He squints until he can almost see the boy he was once upon a time. That kid was a mess but, man, he was also cluelessly cool. Frankie might be struggling to make sense of things, but this he knows for certain: He doesn't miss being young, but he does miss being naïve.

10

CRUMBS.

AS CLAYTON SIPS A CUP of decaf coffee, he savors the quiet moment after the entertaining but rambunctious dinner. Jules's friend Heidi is a handful, to say the least, and he wasn't disappointed when she packed up her boys and boisterousness and left an hour ago. Now, he's enjoying his vantage point from the kitchen counter.

To his left, through the window, he watches Jules and Damon on the deck, their laughter floating in with the evening breeze as they clear away the remnants of dinner. There's a warmth in how Damon looks at Jules, a tenderness that Clayton recognizes all too well. He likes seeing his daughter loved so deeply, cherished in a way every father hopes for. But a pang of unease comes with it, a shadow lurking behind his admiration. It's the same way he looks at Carol, a gaze that holds both adoration and a quiet fear. That kind of love, the all-consuming, soul-deep love that can light up a life, also carries with it the weight of vulnerability. It means giving someone the power to break your heart, to leave you exposed in a way that no amount of caution or experience can guard against. Clayton knows the cost of that kind of love, the risks that come with it, and as much as he's happy to see Jules so loved, he can't help but feel a flicker of apprehension for what the future might hold.

To his right, Clayton can see down the hall into Sophie's bedroom, where a different scene unfolds. Frankie is sitting on the floor, leaning back against the bed, a small smile playing on his lips as he watches Sophie twirl around the room, her doll spinning in her hands like a tiny dance partner. There's a calmness in Frankie's posture, a rare ease that Clayton has come to associate with when Frankie is around children. It's as if the weight he carries lifts just a little when he's in their presence and the simple joy of their world allows him a moment's respite from his own troubles. Clayton thinks back to how Frankie was with Shane's kids, how naturally he stepped into the role of a stepfather, and how beautifully he loved them as if they were his own. That kind of love doesn't come without a price, though, and Clayton can see the toll it's taken. The loss of those kids, the abrupt severing of the ties he had built so carefully, is something Frankie carries like a shadow in his eyes, even now as he watches Sophie dance.

"I told your mom I would get you in bed," he hears Frankie say to Sophie. "She'll kill us both if you're still up when she comes in."

Sophie drops her doll with a matter-of-fact shrug. "I'm taking the long way."

Frankie laughs and grabs her around the waist, dropping her onto the bed. She howls with laughter that fills the house, fills the world. Frankie covers her with her blankets and tucks her seven stuffed sleeping buddies around her in just the right order.

Clayton watches Frankie lean down to kiss her goodnight. He sees Sophie say something that catches Frankie off-guard. He sits on the bed beside her and looks down at his hands. Curious, Clayton steps closer, leaning into the hallway, careful to avoid the floorboard that creaks, hoping to hear what happened.

Frankie finally answers her. "No, honey, I'm afraid they can't."

Sophie grumbles. "Why not?"

Frankie takes a slow breath before he continues. "Well, because I don't live with Shane anymore, I don't get to see them."

"Oh," Sophie sighs. "Well, that sucks."

Clayton covers his mouth to keep from busting a laugh as he watches Frankie try to contain his own laughter, glancing away from her to swallow his grin before turning back. "Yes, it does."

He leans down and kisses Sophie's forehead again and starts to leave. Just before he slips out the door, Frankie turns back to her. "How much should I close it?"

She dramatically thinks for a moment, though Clayton knows what she will say. It's what she always says. "Big enough for a kiss," she says, making Clayton smile this side of heartbreak. He and Carol had the same nighttime ritual when Frankie and Jules were kids.

Frankie obliges, closing the door just enough to leave a crack wide enough for his puckered lips. "Good night, Bug," he tells her before heading back to the kitchen.

Clayton steps back into the hallway, landing on the creakiest of the floorboards.

"Dad, you're not fooling anyone," Frankie says with a small smile. "You were never very good at hiding."

Clayton smiles as Frankie joins him in the kitchen. "I guess you're right. Your mother is much better at that stuff than me."

Frankie looks trapped behind a forced smile. "Yes, I guess she was, er … is."

Frankie's recognition that he's fumbling his words is salvaged by Jules and Damon coming inside, balancing the remaining plates and pans from the deck, and Frankie takes the stack of plates from Jules. He stacks them in the sink and turns on the water. Clayton rolls up his sleeves and moves in, but Jules stops him.

"No, Dad," she says. "Don't do the dishes. I'll do them."

"I don't mind doing them."

Damon wraps his arms around Jules from behind and rests his head on her shoulder, peeking around her hair to Clayton as he gently rocks her back and forth. "Don't waste your time, Clayton. If you do them, she's only going to do them again."

Jules swats him off her and pulls her hair up into a loose knot tied off with a band she pulls from her wrist. "I'd let my dad do the dishes sooner than you. Because he knows how. You don't."

Damon continues to tease her as he swigs off the beer

bottle he pulls from his back pocket. "You leave one crumb, just one time …"

Jules laughs and shakes a fist at him. "A crumb?! Damon, you don't seem to realize that if you stack plates after a spaghetti dinner, you also have to wash the bottoms of the plates."

Damon shrugs. "One time."

"Not one time," Jules says. "That's the problem, dear Damon. Will you please make sure the grill is off?"

Damon rolls his eyes and ducks back outside. Clayton is enjoying their banter, remembering the way he and Carol used to do the same. It makes him grateful to know that she's returning on Sunday. She has been missed.

Frankie doesn't seem as charmed by their exchange, and he pops the top back on the bottle of whiskey. "Well, I'm going. Thanks for dinner."

"Will we see you in the morning?" Jules asks him.

"Of course."

Jules shakes her head. "Don't say 'of course' when you've been blowing off everything else recently."

Frankie bites his lip and starts for the door. "Real nice. I'll see you tomorrow."

"Can't wait," Jules replies with a tone indicating the opposite.

After Frankie leaves, Clayton pats Jules on the back as a mild scold. She turns to face her father. "What? I get that he's hurting, but it's exhausting. And we're left picking up the pieces. I'm running his café. You're housing his broken heart. Hurt happens, but so does life. When will Frankie finally pull it together?"

Clayton brushes the hair out of her eyes and tucks it behind her ear like he's seen Carol do a thousand times. "He will. When your mother is back on Sunday, things will start to get back on track."

Jules pats him on the chest as if to warn him that she has something to say, but before she can start in with something he doesn't want to hear, he cuts her off. "Well, I should be going, too. There are still a few things to do before the market tomorrow."

He starts down the hall, but she grabs his arm and turns him back to her, "Dad."

Dammit, not her, too. "What?"

He looks at his willful daughter, his eyes narrowing as he dares her to question what he knows to be true. A spark in her gaze reminds him of Carol, the very woman they're all angry with right now. But he's not swayed by Jules's unspoken challenge; he's been through this too many times to believe that anything will truly change. His wife—her mother—is coming home on Sunday, just like she always does. They can be mad at her all they want, but those feelings will fade away when she walks through the door again, just like they did the last time and the time before that. Why is everyone pretending this time is different just because she's been gone longer than before?

He wishes he could make Jules see that some things never change. This is who her mother is and has always been. And just like before, she is coming home. She has to be coming home.

"Do you need anything?" Jules asks, patting his arm and handing him a small container of leftovers.

It's a loaded question and he's tired of letting everyone off the hook, so he decides to be honest. "Yes, I need you to believe that your mother is coming on Sunday."

Jules's eyes flicker with sudden tears and she pales a bit in the face of his candor. She studies his face for a moment, probably looking for a weakness in his resolution that she isn't going to find. "Okay," she finally says, and he almost believes her.

"Thank you," he says. "By the way, do you have any Christmas lights? I don't have all the decorations out yet. She'll be so disappointed if they're not up when she gets back."

"Does anyone still do Christmas in July?" she asks, the question tinged with so much more.

"We do," he reminds her, and she nods, pulling him into a hug.

"Okay," she says into his chest.

She starts to pull away, but he tightens his grip, holding her close for just a moment longer. It hits him then, how long it's been since they've shared a hug like this. The last time was the day he got the letter from Carol. He knows something is different about the letter this time, but he's not ready to face what that difference might be. He refuses to consider the alternatives because then the brick house of his life would turn to glass. In holding Jules now, Clayton can feel that the armor that shines around her may be more porcelain than steel. Maybe that's why Jules has been afraid to hug him since the day of the letter; she's afraid the embrace might shatter them both.

He pretends not to notice her wipe away tears as she steps back.

"If Frankie doesn't show up tomorrow, do I have permission to kill him?" she asks, her voice cracking just slightly, betraying the mix of frustration and helplessness she's trying so hard to mask.

"Sure, Sweetie," he says as he turns toward the door, forcing a lightness into his tone that he doesn't quite feel. "You can kill him. Kill him dead."

"Thanks, Daddy," she says as she walks him out. "Cuz I will."

"Oh, my sweet girl," he says as he steps into the evening light. "I have no doubt."

He hears her laugh softly behind him, and he glances back with a wave and a smile as he crosses to his truck in the driveway. When he reaches the truck, he pauses, turning to take in the sight of his fierce daughter standing on the front stoop, her arms crossed, her stance firm. A sudden wave of love swells within him, so strong it nearly chokes him. How could Carol choose to miss this? The question reverberates through him, dislodging a realization he had somehow buried in the chaos of her absence.

For so long, his focus had been on his own sense of loss, on how much he missed her, on the hope that maybe—just maybe—she was out there finding what she needed to come back whole. He had tried to juggle the pieces she left behind to make sense of the wreckage of her decision, but he had never really let himself acknowledge the simple, painful truth: Her leaving was a choice. Each time she had done this, she dressed it up as a calling, as if she were powerless against the pull to explore, to seek out something beyond their life together. He had clung to that explanation, used it to soften the blow, to forgive her absences. But now, standing here, with the weight of his daughter's gaze grounding him, he sees the excuse for what it was—a way for Carol to absolve herself of the responsibility, to place the burden of her choices on something other than herself.

The realization cuts deep. It's not just that he misses her; she chose to miss them. She chose to miss out on the moments that make up a life—moments like tonight that were filled with so much relaxed brilliance. He feels the weight of that choice pressing down on him, the undeniable truth that her leaving wasn't just something that happened to them; it was something she did. And with that truth comes a clarity that's hard to deny. He loved his wife, but her absence was as much a part of her as her presence ever was.

11

DANCE.

JULES RARELY USES THE dishwasher. Instead, she embraces the task manually. She has never admitted to it because it feels like a dirty secret, but Jules loves to do dishes by hand. There's a messy stack to her right that she submerges, one by one, in the hot, soapy water and vigorously scrubs away the caked-on remains of a meal. The plates are restaurant white. Simple. Plain. Void of any design or embellishments. Damon thinks it is because she enjoys plating food, and the unadorned plate creates the perfect canvas for the meal as presented. She goes along with this perception instead of admitting that she simply loves a perfectly clean plate.

The house is quiet after everyone has left, a welcome reprieve from the noise of the evening. Even louder than the conversation around the table were all the unsaid things whispered in glances, in distractions, in the pauses between questions and answers. The conversations with Frankie and Clayton left her a little shaken, both so sweetly fragile that it hurt her teeth. She loves them completely, but she's glad they've taken their tricky neediness elsewhere. Frankie mentioned how difficult it must have been for her to see Joshua, but he just as quickly pulled the attention back to himself. What would she have said if he'd actually kept her reunion with Joshua in the spotlight?

And her father? Demanding she join in his delusion that her mother was returning on Sunday? It had been easier to nod than to push back, but was that ultimately the kindest response? What if she had told him how she really felt about it, about her? That, of course, would be easier if she had a clearer understanding of how she actually felt about these things. The last few months have become blurry from survival tactics. Thank God she has the escape of her husband and daughter to sink her focus into when the rest of it gets to be too much. She knew her father and brother didn't have such escapes, so she was trying to give them grace, but … Fuck. Men can be such babies.

When did she become the caretaker of everyone's emotions? Was it after their mother left, or had she always been the one to smooth over the rough edges and to make sure things didn't fall apart? She thinks back to when they were younger, how she stepped up when her mother decided to go to Seattle for six weeks to study biodynamic farming. At thirteen, Jules felt responsible for the men in her family in her mother's absence, so she taught herself to cook and iron and drive the smaller tractor. Frankie and Clayton told her that she didn't have to take on so much, but they didn't take any of the responsibilities from her. And when her mother returned, even she didn't ease the tasks that Jules had taken on. "Wow, looks like you've got this under control," her mother said, leaving her to clean the chicken and figure out how hot the grease should get to fry up the skin to the kind of crispy that got whistles of appreciation from her dad.

She's thinking about her mother now and has to step away from the sink, afraid that her thoughts might lead her to slide her hand along a knife's blade absentmindedly. The cut of her mother's exit was deep enough—she didn't need any more wounds to remind her of the pain. The kitchen, once her refuge, now feels too exposed, so she moves over to the sofa and settles into the cushions without bothering to turn on the lamp. The neighbor's back patio light filters in through the window, casting soft shadows that feel more comforting than the harsh reality of bright light.

Frankie's words about how he needed to blame her because it was easier than missing Shane and his kids echoed in her mind. She knows all too well the relief that comes from focusing on something—someone—else. She's become a master at compartmentalizing, at turning her mother's absence into a neat series of facts rather than an overwhelming sea of emotions. But sitting here now, in the quiet and the dark, she lets herself feel the hurt she's been pushing away for so long. She digs past the numbness, searching for something raw and real until she finds it—the sharp edges of resentment and abandonment hidden just beneath the surface. She uses them to chip away at the resilience she's built up, letting herself be vulnerable and acknowledge that maybe, just maybe, it's okay to let it be awful for a while. Frankie certainly thought so. Why should he be the only one allowed to wallow?

She closes her eyes and leans back, turning her face toward the window and the faint glow of the neighbor's light as she allows herself to do something she rarely does—she imagines where her mother might be this very moment. She pictures her on a sunlit piazza overlooking the sea, in some tiny coastal town in Greece, her silver hair caught in the breeze, tendrils dancing around her face. She's laughing with the locals, their conversation a patchwork of broken English and hand gestures, and she's wearing the seashell-patterned sundress Jules bought her for Mother's Day years ago, along with the emerald shawl Jules knit for her another year. She imagines her mother lifting the shawl to her face, breathing in the scent of home, a fleeting reminder of the life she left behind.

But as the image sharpens, Jules realizes she's no longer picturing her mother—she's picturing herself. It's her standing on that piazza, her hair tousled by the wind, her shawl draped over her shoulders. And suddenly, there's a hand on hers, warm and familiar. She turns, and it's Joshua, smiling at her with that easy grin that always made her feel like everything might be okay. He pulls her toward him, and she pulls back, not only from him but from the fantasy altogether.

She returns her focus to the room around her, taking in the familiar clutter of Sophie's toys stacked precariously in the corner, the firewood by the fireplace waiting for the first crisp autumn night, and the bookshelf overflowing with stories she has yet to read. She crosses over to the bookshelf and picks up a dusty frame holding two family photos, her fingers tracing the edges as she studies them.

On one side is her childhood family—she's ten, Frankie is

fourteen, and both of them are awkward and uncomfortable in their skin, forcing smiles between their parents. The photograph feels staged, a moment frozen in time where everyone is pretending everything is okay. For the first time, she notices that everyone is looking at the camera except her mother, whose focus is pulled slightly away from center as if something off in the distance had caught her attention at the last second. Jules touches the photo as if trying to get her mother's attention, an absurd gesture that makes her groan.

The other photograph is of her, Damon, and Sophie. They're standing in a sunflower garden, each reacting comically to the oversized flower heads that shoulder their way into the photo as if they, too, want to be part of the memory. It's a picture full of life and laughter, a stark contrast to the rigid smiles in the first photo. Her mother took this picture a couple of years ago as part of a course she was taking at the community college, and it won a blue ribbon at the state fair. "Of course it did," her mother said. "But it's not the picture that won; it's what the picture made people feel that won. I can take credit for capturing it, but you created it."

Jules studies herself in both pictures, trying to make sense of the throughline between the little girl on the left and the woman on the right, and how they both live in the body standing here now, holding these moments in time. The girl in the first photo was already learning to hide her true feelings behind a forced smile to keep up appearances for the sake of peace. The woman in the second photo is genuinely laughing, surrounded by the family she's worked so hard to build, yet there's a flicker of that same guardedness, a need to protect what she has, to keep it safe from abandonment.

She notices the way Damon is laughing so hard and wide that you can see the crooked tooth next to his front teeth, the one that usually makes him so self-conscious that he resorts to a lopsided smile that hides that side of his mouth. That would be one of her mother's gifts, making you feel safe enough to let your guard down and then forcing you to find joy in your insecurities. Jules feels a pang of something she can't quite name—gratitude, perhaps, that her mother froze this moment in time and handed it to her to cherish. But there's also an undercurrent of sadness with the recognition of her mother's ability to make even happy memories feel tinged with uncertainty.

Jules sets the frame back on the shelf, her fingers lingering on the edge. She takes a deep breath and steps back, her eyes drifting to the overflowing bookshelf, to the toys Sophie will soon scatter across the room. The present is here, solid and real, and for now, that's enough.

As she heads back to the kitchen to finish the dishes, she hears Damon cough somewhere down the hall, and she knows he's propped up in bed, reading whatever historical biography has become his current obsession. Or maybe he's traded a book for his laptop to get some work done. His firm is bidding to design a new housing development on the west side of town. Jules is as supportive as she can be, but when she thinks about his behavior during the last development project they landed, she's secretly hoping they don't get it.

He's a phenomenal architect, but the business aspect overwhelms him. Though he won't admit it, Jules has witnessed how Damon gets worried and unhinged during the development process as he navigates the hand-shaking, the parties, the political laughter, and the promises that may or may not be possible. Even while building their own home, she detected a change when he had to transition from the daydream on paper to bringing it to life. He becomes quick to doubt, second-guess, redesign, question. But instead of admitting his insecurities, he projects them onto others by micromanaging and arguing with builders who are doing exactly what they were told to do.

He's not comfortable being vulnerable, not like …

She shuts off the water and shakes off her hands, forcing herself not to think about him. But she can't help it. He defined her teenage years. She thinks back to being fifteen and climbing into his dad's old Ford pickup, knowing her parents would be so pissed if they knew where she was going, what she was doing. But it wasn't the stuff they did that made her feel like a rebel; it was the stuff they talked about. Running away. Going to Nashville or New York City or Hollywood. Some place where dreamers could dream. It was decided: He was going to be a rock star, and she was going to be his manager. Neither knew exactly what that meant, but they did know that she liked to be the boss and that it meant they'd always be together, so it seemed perfect.

"Hey," Damon says, bringing her out of her daydream as he comes into the kitchen. "Isn't this your friend?"

Joshua's sweet baritone slams into her as Damon clicks on the radio, and Jules drops a coffee mug into the empty side of the sink. Her mind says, *you've got to be kidding me*, but she forces herself to respond, "Yep, it sure is."

She picks up the coffee mug, Damon's favorite: an oversized mug decorated with a round cartoon head filled with coffee to the eyeballs with "Almost enough" in a thought bubble. She now notices a crack in the handle. Was it there before, or did it just happen when she dropped it? For some reason, it breaks her heart, and she feels herself getting teary.

Damon saddles up beside her with a soft sway in his hips. "Care to dance, lil' lady?"

He takes her by the hand, and she lets him, but she resists Damon pulling her in too close for fear he will feel the way her heart is pounding against her chest. She hears Joshua's latest single, an up-tempo number called "Like We Used to Do," but she refuses to pay too close attention to the words in front of Damon, fearing she might recognize herself in the lyrics. So instead, she lets her ears go lazy, only hearing the melody as she lets her husband dance her around the kitchen.

She looks at Damon, and she knows she loves him. She really does, but at the same time, she's thinking about that piazza in Greece and a different set of hands pulling her in to dance.

12

HOME.

FRANKIE HAD EVERY INTENTION of driving to his dad's house. But now he's sitting in the middle of the street outside the house he'd lived in with Shane. Before she scurried away, probably to cyberstalk Joshua, Frankie had pulled Heidi to the side. He'd been quietly obsessing ever since she mentioned getting her real estate license. He saw her eyes light up at the prospect of a potential client, but that light dimmed when he asked about Shane's house. She pulled out her phone and made a couple of taps before confirming that the house was currently vacant.

"Well, well, well," she said. "I guess Shane was a bad boy in more ways than one." She turned her phone to Frankie as if he was supposed to understand what he was looking at. She tapped a chipped nail on a small red box.

"It's not just for sale, it's in foreclosure."

Frankie was stunned. "What? That's not possible."

"The internet doesn't lie," she said, immediately correcting herself. "About this anyway."

"How is that possible?" he asked. "I only moved out six months ago."

She tap-tap-tapped a few more times and clicked her tongue. "And he hasn't made a mortgage payment in four."

"I don't understand. He always acted like he had plenty of money."

She clicked her tongue again and patted him on the cheek. "Oh, sweetie. He obviously lied to you. That can't be shocking at this point, right?"

It was a patronizing remark, but also true.

And now he's sitting in the middle of the street, looking over at the house he used to live in, trying to make sense of how many deceptions those walls overheard and how a seemingly quick stop at home in the middle of the week brought it all down. It doesn't look like a house of cards. In fact, it doesn't look like much of anything. Just another forgettable house on a forgettable street. It's a simple one-story, red brick ranch with white trim. The driveway on the left side leads to a separate garage behind the house. This was one thing Frankie first loved about the house. So many newer houses have the garage jutting out front. This never made sense to Frankie. Who the hell is showing off their garage?

Shane didn't love the house immediately. He wanted an attached garage and a primary bedroom with its own bathroom. Frankie was happy to stay in their apartment and keep looking, but Shane seemed desperate to buy a house. They had looked at several, and he didn't like any of them, but Shane liked the size of the yard of this house. God knows why, as it was an uneven rolling lot that led slightly uphill to the next property. He didn't even like yard work. But they were both drawn to the long open living room and a half-finished walkout basement that was ripe with potential.

In the three years since Shane surprised Frankie with the news that he'd put in an offer that was immediately accepted, they never did much with that potential. They never put in a garden. They never finished the basement or added the front porch. The most they accomplished was painting the bedrooms and tearing the old carpet out of the living room to reveal the hardwood floors that they then never refinished.

Frankie notices that Shane finally bought large planters for the front of the house. He had talked about those stupid planters for months but never bought them, even after Frankie gave him a gift card to a nearby garden shop. Apparently, the gift card hadn't gone to waste, unlike their relationship.

He rolls down the window, wanting to feel even closer to his past life. It is after dark but still humid, and the summer air grabs him by the face. He clicks off the air conditioning in the van and welcomes the assault.

The For Sale sign is swaying gently in the night breeze, and Frankie considers calling Heidi to ask for a tour of the house because it seems a delightful exercise in emotional self-abuse. Not that he needs a guided tour; Frankie knows where the hidden key lives.

Lights from an approaching car bounce off the rearview mirror, and Frankie takes it as a sign to drive on. He heads down the street, but before he realizes it, he is circling around the block. It's a good mile and a half around curved side streets to end up back in front of the house.

This time, Frankie turns into the driveway out of habit.

He realizes what he has done and stares at the double spotlight of his headlights on the garage. He puts the car in reverse and tells himself repeatedly, "Go home, go home, go home."

This isn't his home anymore. It is Shane's and about to become someone else's. And that makes him mad. Shane may have paid for the house, but it was Frankie's home, too. It wasn't fair that his ex could just sell it, was it?

Wait, what about the chairs?

Suddenly, Frankie recalls two modern chairs he had found at the Salvation Army. He had been obsessed with them. They were dark green half-circles that sat on three legs. They were the first pieces of furniture Frankie purchased for his new "forever home" with Shane. Shane made fun of them at first. But one day, Shane bought a long ottoman to complement them. They developed a habit of reading the Sunday paper in these ugly chairs while playing footsie under an old quilt on the ottoman.

Where the hell are the chairs now? Were they still in the house? If so, weren't they his? Or would it be stealing? Now, Frankie was weighing a new strategy. Couldn't he justify entering the house he had lived in before it was sold to make sure nothing of his was accidentally left behind? Like two green chairs? Or one shred of dignity?

Inspired by his bullshit justification, Frankie gets out of the van and knocks on the front door. Heidi said it was empty, but Shane could be there. Cleaning. Or packing. Or blowing the husband of one of his good friends.

Only after he knocks twice does Frankie wake from

his trance and realize where he is standing and what he is doing. Rather than run away, Frankie doubles down on his determination. He holds his ground. He tells himself he has every right to be here, hoping to believe it if he repeats it often enough.

A terrifying thought crosses his mind: What would he actually say if Shane came to the door? He hasn't actually seen him since they broke up. Frankie is embarrassed to remember how he had wanted to get together and talk about how they might fix things, but Shane insisted that he had realized they were in two different relationships, and it wasn't fair to either of them to pretend otherwise. Frankie and Jules went over the next day and packed up all of Frankie's things while Shane was at work. He had left his house key under the welcome mat he was standing on now, waiting for Shane to answer. But he doesn't. No one is here.

Frankie knocks again and waits for a few more moments. He then walks around to the back of the house. With the property on a slope, he can't see into the living room window that faces the backyard. He tries to jump up to see, but it's pointless. Not only can he not get high enough, but the house is completely dark.

Then Frankie realizes something. The curtains are gone. There had been thick curtains on either side of the window and a sheer that covered the window. Shane had always closed the sheer at night. Even though the living room faced the backyard, he hated that someone could look in from outside. If the sheer is gone, that means Shane is gone.

It's true. The house is empty.

Frankie collapses onto the driveway. Numbness had been

his emotional state of choice for the last few months, but part of him had always believed that somehow it was going to work out. He and Shane would fix things. They would have a home again. But now Shane was selling the house without him and moving on with a life that didn't involve Frankie. He didn't even know where Shane was moving to next. And where were his stupid chairs?

He walks over to the garage and tries the door. It's unlocked, and Frankie steps inside, clicking on the light.

A near-empty garage seems like a stupid place to feel heartbroken, but so many small moments happened here. That time Toby screamed in hysterics when he dropped his ice cream while getting out of the van. Or when Brady helped Shane paint the garage and spilled a can of paint on himself. The time Shane and Frankie had impromptu, aggressive sex against the workbench in the middle of the day, leaving the garage door open.

Frankie lingers at the workbench now, resting his hands on the exact place where he had to hold on to keep them from falling over that day. Their combined weight had dented the wood on the bench, something Shane always loved to tap with his thumb whenever they walked by it.

Several small jars line the back of the workbench, and Frankie leans in to grab them, trying to ignore the fact that he is getting an erection—the first in months. The sensation isn't unpleasant, but the memories causing it are. He shakes his knees, trying to send the blood in his groin back to where it belongs. In doing so, his knee rattles a bucket under the workbench, and he reaches down to find a plastic bucket filled with Matchbox cars. There are over 200 of them.

Brady and Toby had been collecting them since they could walk, adding to Shane's childhood collection and the few that Frankie added to the mix. Frankie rummaged through them until he found General Lee from TV's *The Dukes of Hazzard*. Sure, it had a confederate flag on the hood that was justifiably taboo, but the episode entitled "The Ghost of General Lee" opened with Bo and Luke Duke skinny-dipping. This moment in television history sent troubling sparks through young Frankie's body. He clearly remembers his brain screaming, "Get out of the water!" and he knew he was in trouble. General Lee represents his coming out to himself as much as anything.

He tucks the mini car in his pocket and opens a few jars, scattering nuts and bolts and screws until he finds a key. The emergency key. Frankie hid it here, knowing that the odds were good they would eventually get locked out. It happened three times when they lived in the apartment—and all three times when Shane insisted he had brought his keys. Their back-up became to leave the back door unlocked, rendering the secret key obsolete.

Looking at the key now, Frankie feels a fresh hurt. Every step of this ridiculous mission is setting off emotional landmines. But he can't stop. There's a quote by Winston Churchill that he keeps playing in his mind, "If you're going through hell, keep going." He knows he is misinterpreting the intention of the quote on purpose to justify what he is doing.

A moment later, the key slides into the back door and opens it. It all seems much easier than it should be. Self-defeat usually is.

The first thing he notices is the smell. It smelled like

home. The basement level had some water issues when they bought the house, and the slightest hint of mildew never went away. He doesn't turn on the lights, but Frankie can tell that the walls have been painted. When they had bought the house, the walls were dark green and offset by white trim. The design has now been reversed with pale walls and wood trim. He carefully touches it as if it might still be wet, the smell of paint in the air.

He creeps up the stairs to the main level, afraid that at any moment he will find that Shane is still very much here. But the main floor is empty. His breathing echoes off the wood floors in the living room. It seems smaller than he remembered. They'd always struggled to place furniture in this long rectangular room. If the sofa took advantage of the wall of windows facing the backyard, there was no logical place for the television. They tried a new variation every couple of months, but they never figured it out. Apparently, they never figured out a lot of things.

The green chairs are nowhere to be seen.

In the kitchen, the refrigerator has a familiar hum. Frankie leans against it, pressing his cheek to the cool door. When he opens his eyes, fresh tears spill down his cheeks.

One by one, he opens every drawer and cupboard. He finds a collection of to-go menus from nearby restaurants. A few of them he doesn't recognize, and it hurts to know that Shane had tried something new without him. Shane was moving on. How do people do that? Keep walking with all the shattered pieces of their heart in their shoes? Maybe the fact was that Shane wasn't heartbroken. Maybe this was his way out.

Down the hall, Frankie stands in the doorway of what had been the boys' bedroom. He remembers the matching twin beds on either side of the window. Brady's had a Batman bedspread, while Toby slept in a SpongeBob-themed fort of pillows and blankets. He touches the walls, hoping to hear the laughter of the boys giggling with glee as Frankie and Shane take turns trying to read Dr. Seuss's tongue twister *Fox in Socks*.

They had used the room at the end of the hall as an office, which was icy with memories. It was here that Shane had left his email account open one day, and Frankie read his exchanges with other men. They'd fought about it. Shane had insisted that he just enjoyed the flirtation but would never act on it. Frankie tried to believe him, but it created a paranoia that turned out to be no paranoia at all.

Streetlights shine into the primary bedroom, which also smells of fresh paint. The day they had moved in, they painted one wall deep red and the other three blue. Shane had plans for a nautical theme; Frankie should have taken the hint from his partner's obsession with the Titanic. Those colors were gone, replaced with a flat white. Bile crawls to the back of Frankie's throat, remembering that it was in this exact spot that his world turned upside down.

After two days at the farm helping his father process their mother's latest surprise exodus, Frankie came into town to get some groceries and to give Jules the key to the café. Deciding to stop at home to grab a change of clothes, he was surprised to find Shane's car in the driveway in the middle of a Wednesday that usually saw him at work. When he stepped in the front door, he could hear what Shane was doing on his lunch break. For a split second, he tried to convince himself that what he was hearing was porn playing from Shane's computer, though he knew that was a sick kind of wishful thinking. At first, Frankie stepped back to leave, not to interrupt, not to be faced with the truth, but then he stepped forward, each step toward the open bedroom door feeling like a stomp on his own heart.

When Frankie stepped into the exact spot where he's standing now, the first thing he saw was the tattoo of wings stretched across Shane's shoulder blades. He was leaning up, back arched as he was thrusting into whoever owned the legs wrapped around his waist, causing the tattoo to flex and pull. The movement was almost hypnotic, like a majestic bird preparing to take flight.

Shane's jeans were tangled around his knees, boxers half-down, one sneaker still on while the other had tumbled into the pile of someone else's clothes. Grunts and moans filled the space, thick and undeniable, slapping Frankie with the truth he can't unhear. After months of wanting to believe otherwise, there was no denying what was on full-technicolor, pornographic display on the bed Frankie's father had built.

For too long, Frankie had let himself believe those tattooed wings symbolized Shane's strength, his ability to carry them through the hard times. But in that moment, the truth became clear: Shane never saw their love as a safe place to land   he saw it as a cage, and he wanted to be free.

"Goddamn it," Frankie finally said, under his breath, more as a realization that he had to be done pretending that Shane loved him like he wanted to be loved. There are relationships where this might be acceptable, permissible, even encouraged, but Frankie wanted something else. "Goddamn it," he said, louder this time as he walked to the bathroom and tossed things in the small garbage bag he pulled from the can next to the toilet. In the next room, he heard Shane and his fuck buddy fumbling around on the bed, maybe even falling off, which brought a sick smile to Frankie's face. "Good," he thought. "I hope it broke Shane's dick."

Shane came to the bathroom door wrapped in the sweat-soaked bed sheet, his face white, his chest heaving. "Frankie," he said with pleading eyes. "I'm sorry." Frankie felt a hint of hope at hearing this. Unfortunately, Shane didn't stop there. "I didn't think you'd come home yet."

If there were any cracks in Frankie's decision to end this, that stupid remark filled them in. "I don't want to do this anymore," he said, just as he realized he was loading Tums and toothpaste into a garbage bag. "What the hell am I doing?" He dropped the bag into the sink and pushed by Shane.

Shane followed him down the hall toward the front door. "Can we talk about this?"

"Shane," Frankie said, stopping him with a hand against the chest he had fallen asleep on at least 100 times but now felt like a mattress of nails. "this isn't a discussion. It's a decision. I'm done."

Frankie had been proud of what he'd said, but he'd played it back a thousand times since, wondering what might have been salvaged if he'd been more open. All kinds of relationships survived infidelity. Many of their friends, especially gay men, seemed to thrive in open relationships. In giving up on Shane, he was letting go of Shane's kids as well. But the truth was, it was Frankie's love of being invited into fatherhood that repeatedly encouraged him to bend when he wanted to break.

He left Shane standing in the hallway and walked out, stopping for gas station pizza and a six-pack of beer. He called Jules on the drive back to the farm, and when he arrived, it was pretty clear she had relayed some version of this update to their father. Clayton didn't ask any questions, but he met Frankie outside with paper plates and a bottle opener, and they got drunk and food-stuffed at the rickety picnic bench next to the horse barn. Clayton only asked once, "Do you wanna talk about it?" It was obvious that such a conversation would take them into territory neither was comfortable exploring together, and Frankie had openly laughed at the suggestion.

"Do you want me to talk about it?" he asked his father while swigging his beer.

Clayton had to admit that he wasn't equipped. "Not really," he said, and they tapped their beer bottles in a silent toast to the awkwardness of trying.

The next day, Frankie and Jules came back to this house and cleared out as much as he could carry in the stupid minivan. Jules repeatedly threatened to destroy anything belonging to Shane and her blinding rage toward him made Frankie's feel sane by comparison.

There's still a small dent in the hollow core closet door from where Jules kicked it. Frankie opens the closet, and it's empty except for a collection of abandoned hangars. He starts to shut the door, but a shadow in the back gets his attention, and he pulls the string on the closet light, revealing one of Shane's ugly cardigans still hanging on a hook off to the side.

It horribly combines pale green, beige, and light purple. It's ugly as hell, but Frankie slips it on and wears it into the big, empty living room.

It's overwhelming to remember the life that happened here. The laughter, love, and pain.

Frankie fishes the Matchbox car out of his pocket and enjoys the reassuring feel of running his thumb over the small wheels. He slides down onto the floor and sets the car on the hardwood as he leans back against the wall in the living room. He rolls it back and forth a few times, revving it up before letting go and watching it sail across the empty room that used to be his home.

"Vroom."

13

LOST.

CLAYTON'S BREATH COMES in short, panicked gasps as he leans against the kitchen counter, his vision blurring at the edges. His heart pounds in his chest, each beat a hammering reminder of the chaos inside him. This is new—this feeling of losing control, of being overwhelmed by something he can't quite name. He's never had an anxiety attack before, and his initial fear was that he was having a heart attack, but he could tell this wasn't happening in his heart; it was desperate panic in his mind. He's grateful that Frankie called to say he won't be home until late because Clayton doesn't know how he would explain what's going on. He doesn't even understand it himself.

The drive home from Jules's house had been a whirlwind of thoughts, a torrent of emotions swirling in his mind, leaving him oscillating between guilt and anger.

But now, where is it? Where did he put it? Panic tightens

its grip on his chest as he frantically searches the kitchen drawers, his movements growing more frantic with each passing second. Has Frankie found it? Has he shared it with Jules? Has Matches seen it, too?

Clayton's hands shake as he rifles through the same drawers again, trying to keep things orderly because he knows Carol hates chaos. She liked things to be where they were supposed to be, everything in its place. But he can't help it. The panic is driving him, making him reckless. The kitchen, the den, the office—he searches them all.

He stands at the door to Frankie's room for a long time, staring in, trying to see if it could be there. A wave of anger washes over him. How dare Frankie take it. How dare any of them. He tells himself that he'll look one more time in his and Carol's bedroom. If he doesn't find it there, he'll go through Frankie's things. He doesn't have a choice.

His hands tremble as he thumbs through the stack of unpaid bills on the small table next to the bathroom. He even goes through the hall closet, lifting towels and extra rolls of toilet paper, but it's not there. The panic in Clayton's chest grows overwhelming, and he stumbles into his bedroom and collapses on the bed, his legs giving out beneath him. He grips the side of the mattress, trying to force his heart to slow, to relax.

And then he sees it—a small white corner of paper poking out from under the bed. He lunges for it, his chest heaving as he pulls the letter free. Here it is. He holds it in his hands, his fingers tracing the familiar creases, and his whole world calms.

He unfolds the letter, and the sight of Carol's loopy,

loving penmanship instantly soothes his raging nerves. He reads it again as if he hasn't memorized it since the moment he found it. Yes, she's coming home. Of course, she's coming home. It's not written in the words, but it doesn't have to be. He's sure of it.

Clayton lifts the letter to his nose, inhaling deeply, searching for the scent of her perfume. It's starting to fade, but he doesn't mind. She'll be back before her scent is gone.

As he slides the letter back into its hiding place, safely out of reach of his prying children, it dawns on him that this might be the first night he's been alone in the house since he found the note. He tries to remember—certainly, Frankie had gone out with friends at some point or spent the evening with Jules. … Hasn't he?

There's a different kind of quiet at night, and all the silences these days seem to carry new meanings. He's suddenly unsure what to do with himself. Retracing his steps, Clayton resets everything he disturbed in his frantic search. When he reaches Carol's writing desk at the top of the stairs, he opens a drawer and finds a ceramic Santa Claus in swim trunks holding water skis. He pauses, smiling at the wonky, squinting little man and all he represents. He remembers buying this trinket for Carol in honor of their first Christmas in July celebration.

When they were 20, Carol's youngest sister, Patty, had been dating a young man named Billy, who had invited them to his parents' cabin on a lake in northeast Iowa. The cabin sat on a high hill above a cove that opened to the long, narrow, winding lake that felt more like a very still river than a lake.

As a surprise one night, Billy loaded the foursome, a cooler of beer, and a bag of snacks into a boat and introduced them to the local tradition of Christmas in July. The cove is almost dead center in the nine-mile-long lake, so they cruised down one way and then back the entire length before returning to the house. Along the way, house after house was fully decorated for Christmas. Lights and plastic snowmen, reindeer on inner tubes, stars shining from boat docks. Out on the lake was a parade of boats equally festive, and Christmas music echoed off the water. Carol was in awe of it all, giddy with childlike glee. That night, watching the way her face beamed with the purest kind of joy, is the night Clayton fell in love with her.

A year later, back at the lake, but this time without Patty and Billy, Clayton proposed to Carol on a rented boat in the middle of the Christmas in July parade. Two years later, they married on July 25th with a Christmas-themed wedding. Not one to let a good thing go, Carol rallied the neighbors around Clayton's family farm into starting a Christmas in July tradition. All the nearby farms decorated for Christmas and had hayrides and horse-drawn buggy tours. Some years it became a fundraiser for various local charities. Other years it was just for fun. Over the years, after Clayton took over the farm from his parents, it drifted away from tradition until only the Parker house was known for its Christmas in July decorations. It caused much humiliation for Frankie and Jules during their teenage years, as classmates teased them, but Carol always believed they secretly enjoyed the attention. Clayton believed that Carol loved the annual tradition because it happened on their anniversary, making it also a celebration of their wedding. She brushed off the suggestion with such insistence that he knew he wasn't completely off the mark.

Clayton carries the little Santa figurine downstairs to the kitchen and sets it on the windowsill above the sink. As he continues to relax, he realizes that his panic has soaked through his shirt.

He pulls the flannel off and drops it on the kitchen table, drawn to step outside into the evening air in his undershirt. Even that feels constraining, and he pulls it off to stand shirtless, using the shirt as a rag to wipe away the sweat and doubt. A coyote howls in the distance, and he's reminded of what JP had said about how the noises were different in the country. He wasn't wrong.

The air is still thick with humidity, but the darkness has brought a welcome reprieve from the heat. There's even a bit of briskness in the breezes, which finds its way over Clayton's sweaty chest and arms. He moves farther into the yard, walking until the lights of the house are eclipsed by the barn, and the only light comes from the moon above. He looks up at it, hanging there, perfectly round, full, and still among the ocean of stars, and he wonders if it looks as lonely to Carol as it does to him.

He lets his mind drift into the memory of the day before Carol left. It was her birthday, and Frankie closed Fuel Injector to the public for a private party with the family. Carol pretended to be horrified by the cake decorated with 65 candles by Sophie and Frankie's stepsons, Toby and Brady, saying, "Certainly, that's a fire hazard!" Well, almost stepsons. Frankie didn't know it yet, but Shane had pulled Carol aside to whisper that he planned to propose on Valentine's Day. She had told Clayton as much as they took the long way home after the party. When he found her note the next morning, he was sure she'd be back in time for the engagement party. That announcement never came, of course, with the way things ended between Frankie and Shane, and maybe she'd heard it through the grapevine, and that's why she hadn't come home yet.

He walks back toward the house but is pulled to the opposite side of the driveway to where the wild berries are taking ownership of the yard. This is where he'd found the clues of her departure back in January. He'd found the footprints of her boots in the snow, with the boxy imprint of where she had set down her two bags of luggage to turn back and lock the door. She left while he ran into town to get gas for the snowblower. She didn't like to drive in the snow but, apparently, she wasn't the one who drove away. Her car was still in the garage, and the tracks from whoever had picked her up lined the driveway. Clayton hadn't noticed the tracks when he'd returned with the gas. Whoever had been driving had turned around in the small side lot carved out in the gravel for guest parking. They weren't familiar with the driveway because they had obviously run over the flowerbed that framed the driveway. Carol likely had something to say about that, as it had been her longtime obsession to carefully select the flowers that would welcome visitors from the street.

Clayton kicks dirt over the memory, heads back inside where he stands at the kitchen sink and examines the coffee mug that had been the paperweight holding down the letter. He glances at the picture of Carol that hangs in the window nook. He remembers the day Jules took the photo. She had asked her mother to model for her as part of the photography class she was taking in high school. They had gone downtown to the roof of a parking garage. Jules was obsessed with New York at the time and was desperate for industrial backdrops or, really, anything that would allow her to briefly forget she was a farm girl. In this photo, Carol is smiling but not looking at the camera as if she's entertained by something she has seen off to the side. She has always been like that. Looking around for inspiration.

Clayton swigs down some ibuprofen with a glass of water and sets the glass in the sink with a sigh. He clicks off the light as he heads back through the house, climbing the stairs to the empty bed, waiting to be filled with dreams of reconciliation.

SATURDAY

14

SWEAT.

"WHAT'S 'TIT SWEAT?'"

Jules nearly falls off the front porch when she hears Sophie repeat her off-color comment as she waddles sleepily down the hall toward her. It's not yet six in the morning, and Jules has been muttering about how hot it already is, though obviously louder than she realized. She looks over her sunglasses at the child and wonders how to explain. But she's running late to meet Clayton at the farmers' market, so she punts the question to Damon as he appears from the kitchen.

"Daddy can tell you over pancakes. Right, Daddy?"

But Sophie has already lost interest in her question and climbs into Damon's arms, resting her head on his shoulder and rubbing his scruffy chin.

He hands Jules a bottle of sunscreen, but she crinkles her nose. "I already have some on."

"You're a liar." He turns to Sophie. "I think Mama's a liar.

She doesn't smell like coconuts, does she?"

Sophie leans toward Jules and dramatically sniffs. "Nope. She smells like a liar. A liar with tit sweat."

Damon snaps his accusatory eyes at Jules, who bites her lip. "Be good for Daddy today."

Damon winks at Jules. "I think you should be good for Daddy later."

Jules smirks and gives him a quick kiss. "You're holding a child, Pig."

He shrugs it off. "You taught her 'tit sweat' before breakfast. We're even."

It's hard to argue his logic, so she doesn't even try and walks away. "You kids have fun."

"He's not a kid!" Sophie shouts, holding Damon's face. "He's a man!"

Damon lets his expression hint at all the things he'd like to say, and Jules waves a finger warning to zip his lip as he heads back inside.

She pulls open the truck door, and a cloud of heat explodes out like an oven. She gags a bit, swinging the door like a big metal fan as if it would do any good. She slides in and immediately sticks to the leather seats, cursing under her breath as she turns on the engine. A burst of air from the air conditioner blows back her hair. So does Joshua's smooth voice, serenading her from the radio. She snaps off the air conditioner and the radio with a single desperate swipe of her hand. Really, does the radio only have access to his music these days? Jules's eyes dart around to see if anyone saw her listening to his song.

Wait, why the shame? Nothing is happening. He's her

high school boyfriend, and they're still friends. That's not a dirty secret. He's a local boy chasing a dream that got him on the radio. That's not a secret. He's back in town. That's not a secret. She masturbated in the kitchen this morning, thinking about him while the coffee took its sweet-ass time brewing.

Okay, that part is a secret.

She leans back in the seat and covers her mouth with her hand as if she's trying to keep her secret from the air freshener dangling from the mirror or the fast-food containers on the passenger floor. Realizing she's covering her mouth with the same hand she used to … remember him this morning, she wipes it on her jeans. Even though she has showered since, it still represents regret that she'd rather not hold to her lips.

"Stop it," she scolds herself in the rearview mirror. She doesn't trust the eyes of the woman looking back at her, so she drives downtown, treating speed bumps like fistfights. She hits back because she can and also because it shakes her up a bit.

Even at this early hour, the downtown farmers' market is buzzing with people and energy as the various vendors set up shop along the streets. Jules parks in her usual spot under the skywalk next to her father's truck. Matches's pickup is in Frankie's usual spot. Well, it was his usual spot until he started taking more morning shifts at the warehouse on weekends to dig his hole of solitude even deeper. Jules is fascinated by how Frankie has managed to use one kind of responsibility as a weapon against another kind of responsibility. That's a skill she doesn't have. Like her mother, she feels all in or all out when it comes to the responsible thing. She pictures Frankie sitting on the floor of the empty warehouse, sipping coffee in the air conditioning while she sweats her ass off dealing with the public as she helps her dad rid their booth of their fruits and vegetables.

Matches knocks on her window, pulling Jules out of the daydream of punching Frankie repeatedly in the face. She smiles and opens the door to be met by Matches handing her sunscreen. She won't take it from Damon, but from Matches, she does. Realizing this, she wonders if she's mad at Damon for some reason. Maybe she's mad at him for not being more perceptive to the fact that Joshua has planted himself in the center of her mind. She feels guilty for the way she casually thinks of him, wonders about his life on the road, and can feel him thinking about her from across town.

Joshua. Joshua. Joshua.

Stop it.

Matches is talking about green bean salad when Jules is pulled back into their conversation by Matches working sunscreen into Jules's arms in an awkward but soothing kind of massage.

"… and then I realized I was out of balsamic vinegar, so I improvised with red wine vinegar, and it was definitely different, but fine. Remind me to swing by Elsa's stand before I leave to see if she has any balsamic."

Jules realizes she's wearing the facial expression of a corpse and pulls on a smile. "Will do."

Matches smiles and pats her on the arms as if to say, "I know you weren't listening, and that's okay. Life's a mess, and I am rambling about friggin' green bean salad. I get it."

Jules wants to care about the green beans, but Matches

has moved on. "Think Frankie will show up today?"

"For his own physical well-being, I hope so," Jules says as Pete comes up to fetch a pallet of tomatoes off the back of their truck. As he hoists it up, he throws Jules a "good morning" as he teeters away. JP takes Pete's place to get the second pallet, glancing at Jules and immediately blushing in all his teenage glory.

Jules knows JP has a crush on her, and it makes her feel good. Maybe she's not a horrible person for having nonstop, filthy thoughts about Joshua. Maybe she can make amends by being a good old-fashioned cradle-robbing slut. "Well, JP. Hello, you little devil. Though you're not so little anymore, are you? Damn."

She takes the sunscreen from Matches with a wink and holds it out to JP. "Can you be a doll and put this on my back? I always ignore my backside and pay for it later."

JP turns bright red and stutters, "I … uhh … corn."

He scurries away as Matches cackles. "Oh, that poor boy has loved you since he was in diapers. Just ask your mother—"

The statement crashes between them like an iceberg. Matches looks like she might die from embarrassment. "Shoot. I'm sorry. I—"

Clayton scoots up to Matches's truck and grabs another pallet of tomatoes, mumbling about JP's odd behavior until he sees Jules. "That explains it. You're here."

"Of course, I'm here. I'm always here. Unlike some people."

Clayton glares at her. "Leave your brother alone. He left a message last night that he's going to be here."

He makes his way back into the farmers' market and Jules swings the door shut on her truck, asking aloud, "Wait. Left a message last night? Didn't Frankie come home?"

Matches shrugs and starts away before turning back to Jules. "I should probably let it go, but it will haunt me all day if I don't apologize for mentioning your mother."

It may have been annoying at another time, but it didn't matter today. "Let it go. We've got better things to talk about. Like green bean salad."

Matches laughs. "So, you were listening!"

"Kinda."

As they make their way through the maze of cars, Matches casually fills the conversation with teaching JP how to play cribbage, how great the tomatoes look this season, gossip about a supposed affair between two vendors near their booth.

They find Clayton, Pete, and JP in the thick of the early morning madness, moving with the practiced ease of doing this a thousand times before. The methodic dance of it all lulls Jules into a delicious active meditation, giving her thoughts a safer place to rest than the flexing they've been doing around Joshua and all he represents. Crates of vegetables are stacked neatly, some already emptied onto the wooden display tables while others wait their turn. The faint smell of freshly turned earth mingles with the sweet scent of ripening tomatoes and the sharp tang of onions.

Jules takes a deep breath, and it's like the whole world narrows down to this single act of preparation. It's a process she knows well, one that has always brought her a sense of peace. She moves to help Pete arrange the heirloom tomatoes, her hands brushing against the smooth, firm skins. They're warm from the morning sun, and their vibrant colors seem to glow against the backdrop of weathered wood.

She glances around as the market begins to hum with life, somehow moving fast and in slow motion at the same time. Other vendors are setting up their stalls, the soft murmur of voices carrying on the breeze. A few early risers wander through the streets even before the market is officially open, clutching steaming cups of coffee, their eyes scanning the displays as they plan their purchases.

The market is a world unto itself, where everything has its proper place, unlike her thoughts recently, which all feel so improper and out of place. Joshua. Joshua. Joshua. His name alone is enough to send a ripple of unease through her, a reminder of things she'd rather leave buried. But here, surrounded by the fruits of her family's labor, she can push those thoughts aside, at least for now.

Jules straightens up, wiping her hands on her jeans, and takes a moment to survey the booth. It's coming together nicely—the rows of carrots, the baskets of peppers and beans, the bundles of leafy greens all carefully arranged. Her dad catches her eye and gives her a quick nod of approval. It's a small gesture, but it warms her. This is where she belongs, in the thick of it, working alongside her family to bring their farm's bounty to market.

As the last of the crates are emptied and the booth is finally ready, Jules steps back, letting herself take it all in. The sun is climbing higher now, casting a golden light over the market. The early morning calm is beginning to give way to the busyness of the day, but for now, there's still a quietness, a moment of peace before the crowds arrive.

She turns to help Clayton with the final touches, a small

smile playing at the corners of her lips. Whatever else is going on in her life, whatever thoughts of Joshua or anything else might come later, right now, this is enough.

One final deep breath before they open their booth, the official notice indicated by her father's hand on her shoulder. "Okay," he says. "Here we go."

15

FUCK.

"FUCK FUCK FUCK." Frankie is humming this mantra while standing in the shower. He isn't naked, the water isn't on, and this isn't even his bathroom anymore.

"Hello?" comes a voice from the other side of the shower curtain. It's pink and floral and smells like cheap plastic. Frankie considers eating it to see if it will kill him instantly. Instead, he glances at his watch. Seems like a good time to die. He's still wearing Shane's ugly cardigan; maybe he can quickly unravel the thread and use it to hang himself.

When the curtain is pulled back, Frankie glances at the handsome young man with question-mark eyebrows and turns to the corner of the shower with all the skill of an ostrich trying to hide. "You aren't supposed to be here," says the man, balancing between confusion and amusement.

Frankie has only one thing to say in his defense. "This used to be my home."

A few moments ago, Frankie awoke on the floor in the middle of the living room of the house he once shared with Shane. Somehow, he'd fallen sound asleep on the cold wood floor. His alarm clock had been this man, presumably a real estate agent here to show the property to the equally surprised couple he was leading into the house with their young child in tow. Frankie's response was to startle-fart and then scramble away to hide in the nearest place, which turned out to be the shower.

"Did you know Shane?" asks the man.

Frankie glances toward him, winces, and then turns his focus to a layer of soap scum in the built-in soap dish. "I loved him, but I didn't know him."

"Wait," the man says. "Frankie?"

The recognition enrages Frankie for some reason, and he storms out dramatically. Or he tries to, but instead, he trips over the tub, gets wrapped up in the stupid shower curtain, and then collapses against the real estate agent. They wrestle for a moment, and Frankie gets the sense that the man is laughing. Once liberated from the curtain, Frankie tumbles out of the bathroom, down the hall, and past the couple, clutching their crying child. "Fuck ... sorry sorry sorry," he mumbles as he rushes by them and out the front door, racing to his big, stupid minivan.

He clamors into the van and fumbles as the key refuses to cooperate with his trembling hands. "Get in the hole!" he yells at the key, begging it to find its way into the starter. It ignores him, and instead, the entire key chain swan dives to the floor mat, and he has to smash his face against the steering wheel as he tries to reach for the keys blindly. Turning his head toward the driver's side window, he discovers the real estate agent is standing outside his window, patiently watching him. Frankie pretends not to notice him and certainly isn't going to notice how cute he is, not with the way he's standing there calmly, with a smile clearly tickling the corners of his mouth. Why is he calm? Why is he cute?

"Dammit!" Frankie shouts, hoping it will scare the man off. It doesn't, but at least he's found his keys.

The key does its job, and the engine roars to life, thank God. The man is suddenly less entertained and more frantic as he knocks on the window. "Wait!"

Frankie is a bag of crumbling nerves and frayed emotions, and he's running out of steam, so he does the only thing he can think of doing, which is to scream, "What do you want?!" But he has screamed against a closed window, undermining the effect. Frankie shakes his head in self-disgust, lowers the window, and turns to the man, forcing a demeanor that indicates what is hopefully perceived as sanity despite all indications to the contrary.

"I'm sorry. I'm leaving."

The guy tips his head from side to side, carefully placing the next words down in front of Frankie. "I'm afraid you can't do that yet."

As the man nods sympathetically, Frankie really notices how young and handsome this man is. Because why wouldn't he be? Why couldn't he humiliate himself in front of an old troll? Why does it have to be Bradley Cooper's little brother?

"Fuck," Frankie sighs. "Because you called the cops?"

Now the man is smiling even wider, just short of laughing. "No, because I first want to move my car, which is currently holding the sweet young couple who have probably shit twice in my cup holder."

Frankie turns to see the couple sitting in the back seat of a brand-new Jeep Grand Cherokee, clutching their child. He looks back at the man. "Weren't they just inside?"

"Yeah, they pretty quickly decided this probably isn't the house for them," Handsome Stranger says. "Odds are good, at this point, they've probably decided I'm not the agent for them either."

"Sorry," Frankie says. He looks back at the house in an attempt to help. "It's actually a shitty house."

Handsome Stranger's demeanor shifts to concern. "Are you okay to drive?" He reaches over with a paw of a hand and rests it on Frankie's forearm. It sends a jolt through Frankie's body that is both foreign and familiar. Possibly sensing the unexpected intimacy and Frankie's reaction, Handsome Stranger pulls his hand away. "Sorry."

"No, I'm sorry," Frankie says again. Neither of them moves, and Frankie has to look away from this man's concern, which feels weirdly comfortable. "Where are the green chairs?" he mumbles to himself as if it makes sense. He tries to shake the madness from his ears. "Yes, I'm fine."

Handsome Stranger pats Frankie's arm again and seems to accept this as true. "Groovy," he says, tapping Frankie's arm with a finger before stepping back.

He gives Frankie a little nod and jogs back to his Jeep. Frankie hears muffled yelling from the back seat as the house hunters give Handsome Stranger an earful. Frankie watches in the rearview mirror as the man opens and shuts his mouth, trying to say something, but gets repeatedly interrupted. He seems to catch Frankie's eye in the mirror and shoots him a wide-eyed "What the hell?" with a quick smile before backing his Jeep down the driveway.

Frankie follows suit, slipping his van into reverse. As Handsome Stranger's car pulls away, Frankie notices the window in the back seat roll down, and the little girl reaches out with her hand to wave goodbye to Frankie.

It makes Frankie burst out laughing as he waves back.

Kids are awesome.

16

DONUTS.

THE SUN IS BARELY UP, but the Des Moines Downtown Farmers' Market is already a hive of activity. Clayton stands behind the table loaded with the morning's harvest, mechanically moving his hands as he arranges tomatoes, cucumbers, and bunches of fresh herbs into neat rows. Beside him, Jules huffs about Frankie, her frustration palpable in the early morning air.

"Unbelievable," she mutters, stacking a crate of bell peppers with a little too much force. "Of course, he didn't show up. I told you he wouldn't."

Clayton doesn't respond immediately; instead, he scans the crowd, hoping to find Frankie rushing toward them to help. But all he sees is a sea of faces, some familiar, some strangers, but none of them Frankie's.

"He'll be here," Clayton says finally, though he knows his voice lacks conviction. He doesn't meet Jules's eyes; instead, he focuses on adjusting the zucchini display. "He said he'd be here."

"He says a lot of things," Jules shoots back, her tone sharp. "We're here. He should be, too."

Clayton glances at his daughter, noting the tightness in her expression and the way she bites her lip to keep from saying more. Jules has always been the responsible one, the one who holds things together, even when the world seems to be falling apart. But he knows this situation with Frankie is wearing on her. He feels it, too. It has been difficult for him to learn how to honor a sensitive child, especially a son. It isn't how he was raised. His father would have had a lot of choice words for what he believes Frankie needs, a swift kick in the ass likely at the top of the shortlist. Carol taught Clayton to think differently, but in her absence, he feels the pull to respond the old-fashioned way.

Matches slides in beside Clayton, helping JP arrange jars of homemade preserves and honey they've spent the last few months working on. Pete whispers something to Matches that makes her blush and swat him away. Clayton envies their ease, missing the similar interactions he'd be having with Carol if she were here. The farmers' market is one more thing that makes him miss her. She was the one who first dragged them all to the market years ago. After they'd been there the first time as patrons, she insisted they get their own booth the following summer, and she spent the next year planning. She interviewed other booth owners about best practices and things their experience had taught them. She ordered the right tables, awning, and signage. She got all the right licenses and registrations. It took Clayton a while to get into the spirit of it all, but Carol immediately loved it—the energy, the community, the business of caring. Even when the kids were little, she made it a family affair, insisting they all take part. And now, even though she's off on another one of her "adventures," as she calls them, the market is still as much hers as it is theirs.

He sighs, rubbing a hand over his face. Missing her is starting to feel exhausting. He needs her presence, her spirit. The way she could take something as mundane as a farmers' market and turn it into something vibrant, something special. But she isn't here, and he has to keep things going. For the family, for the farm.

"Things are still slow. Go for a walk," Matches says, reading him like she always can. "Get some coffee."

"No, I'm fine," Clayton replies, though the weariness in his voice betrays him, and he reconsiders. "Are you sure you wouldn't mind?"

Matches responds by pushing him out of the booth. "Bring me back a donut."

Clayton gives a small, grateful smile as he steps away from the booth, adjusting the brim of his cap as he moves through the growing crowd. He flexes his hands to release the tension that's becoming more common in his fingers, then drops them into his pockets, trying to shake off the exhaustion that clings to him like a second skin.

The market is in full swing now, with vendors calling out their prices and customers chatting and laughing as they peruse the stalls. Clayton makes his way through the familiar maze of booths, his mind only half on finding coffee. The other half is still back at the booth and the nagging worry hanging over him like a cloud.

He knows Jules is right—Frankie should be here. Should have shown up to help, to pull his weight, to be part of the family. But Clayton also knows that his son is struggling in ways that Jules can't understand. Ways that Clayton himself struggles to understand. It isn't just the breakup; it's everything that came before it—the weight of expectations, the pressure to be something he isn't, the lingering sadness that Clayton can see in Frankie's eyes but can't seem to reach. Only Carol seems to be able to get through to him in that magical way of a mother.

As he approaches his favorite coffee stand, Clayton's mind drifts back to when Frankie was a little boy. Back then, everything seemed so much simpler. Frankie was sensitive, sure, but he was also full of life, curious, and eager to learn. Clayton tried to nurture that, to be the kind of father who encouraged rather than disciplined, but it hasn't always been easy. Carol pushed him to be softer, to listen more, to understand. And he tried—God, how he tried. But now, with Carol gone, he can't tell if the chasm between him and Frankie is growing or shrinking.

The line at the coffee stand is long, but Clayton doesn't mind the wait. It gives him a chance to gather his thoughts and figure out what he's going to say to Frankie when he finally shows up. If he shows up.

"Clayton?" a voice pulls him from his thoughts, and he turns to see his neighbor, Old Man Dotzell, who, truth be told, is a year younger than Clayton but looks two decades older. Three wives, a cancer scare, and a season of fungal disease that took three cropless years to recover from will do that to a person. They exchange pleasantries and talk about the weather, the market, and the new neighbors moving in across from them both, but all the while, Clayton's mind is elsewhere. He barely notices when the conversation ends, and it's his turn to order, but before he can, he hears another, even more familiar, voice.

"Hey, Dad." Clayton turns as Frankie moves up beside him. "Let me get it."

Clayton studies his son as Frankie orders two coffees and a box of donuts. Frankie looks exhausted, with bags under his eyes and his face scruffier than usual. His usually buzzed hair has grown out a bit and is a bit matted, as close to bedhead as hair like that can accomplish. He's also coated in a thin layer of sweat, no doubt because he's wearing a thick cardigan more appropriate for mid-December than late July.

He catches Frankie noticing his sweater, and Frankie shrugs, handing his father a coffee. "Don't ask."

"I wasn't going to," Clayton says. "But Jules will likely have something to say about it."

Frankie responds by rolling his eyes, a response to his sister Clayton has seen a hundred times. "I can't promise she and I won't throw punches today."

"Try," Clayton responds as they step out of line and head back toward their booth.

They walk back in silence, the only sound between them the rustle of the donuts in the box and the murmur of the market. Clayton tries to imagine what Carol might say to him at this moment, but everything that comes to him feels prickly on his tongue like it would come out wrong or insincere. Every time he glances at Frankie, he finds him looking away, lost in thoughts that feel disrespectful to interrupt.

"Ugh," Frankie says suddenly, noticing something ahead. "Mom hates bikes at the farmers' market."

Clayton is surprised by the mention of Carol. She's rarely discussed, especially so casually or with this hint of an enjoyable memory at her sometimes-raucous proclamations. Frankie tips his chin, indicating what inspired the comment, and Clayton notices a family of four ahead, three of them on bicycles with a baby strapped into a child's seat behind the father's seat and a snaggle-toothed boxerdoodle in a seat behind the mother's seat. They are walking their bikes next to each other, taking up an obnoxious amount of space that forces other people to walk around them.

A memory brings a short laugh to Clayton's lips, and Frankie glances at him over his coffee cup. "What?"

"You know what she would call them, don't you?" Clayton says, enjoying how it sends a sparkle into Frankie's eyes.

"Twats," they say in unison, loud enough for the bike mother to look their way. Clayton responds by raising his cup to her in a way that may as well be a middle finger. "Good morning."

17

PLASTIC.

JULES ACCIDENTALLY CRUSHES a perfectly good tomato in a subconscious response to seeing Frankie make his way through the market crowd, laughing beside their father. The meditative calm she had felt before the market opened is replaced by the jagged frenzy of being overstimulated and under-hydrated, and Frankie's laissez-faire approach was infuriating. He's late, of course. Looks like shit, of course. He's also bringing donuts to share with everyone, so he's also everyone's savior. Of course. And, for God knows what reason, he is wearing a ridiculously ugly wool cardigan in the blazing heat. Sometimes, he makes her want to scream.

She rinses the seedy tomato guts from her hand with bottled water that should instead be quenching her thirst. She shakes the water off in Frankie's direction, and he wipes off his face as he dips under the awning of their booth, saying good morning to everyone else but pointedly ignoring Jules.

He's not an idiot. He knows she is pissed. Well, maybe he is an idiot because when his offer for a donut is ignored, he asks, "Why are you mad? I'm here, aren't I?"

The list of reasons is lengthy and ridiculous, but she starts with the obvious. "You're late. And you look like an asshole. Lose the sweater. It's going to be 100 degrees in 10 minutes."

She should be done chewing him out, but she's not. "You're responsible for the teardown. I'm not doing that, too. I set all this up. I'm leaving as soon as we shut down."

"Fine," he says. "Why wait? Go now. You've done a lot. I get it."

His acknowledgment is so unexpected that she doesn't know what to do with herself other than shift her nitpicking into teasing. "Other than that horrible sweater, I'd swear that's the same thing you were wearing last night at dinner. Dad said you didn't show up last night. What is this? A walk of shame, perhaps?"

Frankie slips her a side eye while bagging some tomatoes for Mrs. Wrecken, a walking bag of tomatoes herself with her rosy skin, unnaturally red hair, and a green ribbon in her hair. "You're not wrong, but you're also not right," he says as he moves around her to the cashbox.

The comment is too much of an invitation. On any other day, she might consider letting it go based on the sharp corners of his mood. But not this morning. His uneasiness lights a fuse on her saltiness.

"Was it Bobby?"

This finally gets Frankie's full attention, and he turns to her, exasperated. "Who?"

The fact that he doesn't know who she means is absurd.

He can't possibly be serious. "Office Bobby. Duh."

Mrs. Wrecken has eaten all the watermelon samples and moved to the sugar snap peas. She's staring at Frankie while she eats them, like a dare, one hand on her hip, the other feeding her maw. He stares back at her, reaching over to grab a pea for himself and biting into it like a vampire. Still staring at the forager, he responds to Jules out of the side of his mouth, "You're an idiot. Bobby isn't gay."

But his volume was too loud. Mrs. Wrecken's eyebrows race for her hairline as she looks at him as if they're in the middle of a conversation rather than glaring at each other over food samples. "Who's Bobby?" she asks, reaching for one of the free strawberries.

Jules grabs her own strawberry, leaning toward Mrs. Wrecken as if they are old friends. "Bobby is Frankie's boss," she explains, which gets a vacant nod from the old woman. Then Jules adds, "And he would wear his knees like earrings if Frankie asked him to."

Mrs. Wrecken gasps and pulls her face into a knot before she scurries away, taking the rest of the strawberry samples, paper bowl and all. Despite himself, Frankie chuckles. One point for Jules.

"Why would you say that?" he asks. "Have you ever met Bobby?"

"Yes," she responds, punching him in the arm. "How many times did I drop lunch off at your office? Have you met him?"

Frankie stares at her like she's got two heads, and it makes no sense to her that he could be that oblivious. "Wait, you're serious? Not only is he gay with a capital G, but he's very much interested in taking you to lunch, if you know what I mean."

"Yes," he grumbles. "I know what you mean." She starts to give him a further definition that he doesn't need, but he gets pulled away briefly to help a timid-looking man understand the difference between beefsteak and Roma tomatoes. His wife is waiting for him a few booths down; he got it wrong last weekend. He'd rather not make that same mistake again. Frankie saves the poor man from any potential wrath and sends him on his way with a few sprigs of herbs as a free gift with purchase.

Clayton leans between his kids, his frustration making his voice shake. "What did you say to Mrs. Wrecken? She's one of our best customers, ya know."

Jules resorts to an old classic. "Frankie did it."

Clayton shakes his head, scolding them as if they were children. "Be nice. To each other and the customers. If you can't do that, leave now."

He turns his attention to the arrival of a young family juggling a bucketful of toddlers. Jules turns back to Frankie, hoping to find some new scab to pick at, but finds Frankie crouched down behind their table. At first, she thinks he dropped something, but then he peeks over the table into the crowd and ducks down again. "What are you—"

Frankie slaps her with dagger eyes and rises halfway from a crouch to scan the crowd again. Jules follows his eyeline. In a sea of a thousand bodies, it's clear who he's looking at.

"Holy shit. Did you sleep with Hugo Carson?"

The mention of the name sends Frankie to his feet and out of the tent, where he disappears into the vendor parking lot. Of course, she follows him. Both of them ignore Clayton, yelling after them to get back to work.

"You know him?" Frankie throws over his shoulder, swaying his hips back and forth as he dodges side mirrors in the tightly cramped parking area while slipping off his sweater.

"Work the runway, Princess."

Frankie stops and turns back to her. "Shut up and tell me if you know him."

It's weirdly enjoyable for Jules to be poking this particular bear. "Make up your mind; should I shut up or tell you if I know him?"

Frankie's energy swings like a punch, and she takes the hint to step down. For now. "I own, technically, you own, the only gay coffee shop in town. Of course, I know him. He's a real estate agent."

He grumbles something under his breath and stretches up on his toes to scan the crowd again. This seems to Jules like as good an invitation as any, so she sings "Frankie and Hugo, sitting in a tree. F. U.C.K.I.N.G."

He throws an invisible rock at her and starts away. "I hate you."

Jules suddenly realizes she's having way more fun than she should. But she can't help adding, "Explains why your breath smells like an asshole sandwich. Stop by Judy's booth and suck on some mint leaves, wouldja?"

She follows him back to their father's tent, where Frankie tries to busy himself with the next customer. Jules stands uncomfortably close to him, forcing her way into his dance space with a porn star's grin. "Is he the first since Shithead?"

There's a tornado happening inside Frankie, and Jules is dying to be Toto. He calms for a moment and looks at her. "It's not what you think."

Frankie moves away from her and crash-lands in front of the one and only Hugo Carson, who has come to stand at the table. Jules yelps and possibly even pees a little as she watches the scene unfold. She's fascinated by the way Frankie, who until recently was known to be criminally cool, appears to suddenly be bouncing off invisible walls while Hugo nonchalantly torments him with his calm demeanor. She gets the feeling that whatever happened between them wasn't sexual but was somehow better. She's starving for details.

"Hey, Jules. How's business?" Hugo smiles at Jules as Frankie swallows an internal scream that can be heard from space.

She fears her smile is so big she resembles a Pez dispenser, and any attempt to thwart it will make her look like a serial killer. "It's entertaining," she manages to squeak out between clenched teeth.

"I'm sure it is." He turns to Frankie, who is pretending to be deep in discussion with Matches, who is actually deep in discussion with Mrs. Welden, who has circled back to the booth, as she always does, hoping for an offer of unsold produce leftovers that would go to waste otherwise. Give an old cat a damaged parsnip one time ... Hugo glances back at Jules and winks as if to say, "Watch this." He taps Frankie, who responds as if he's been electrocuted. Somehow, this makes Jules the happiest she has been in weeks.

"How come I don't see you at Fuel Injector anymore?" Hugo asks Frankie. As Jules watches him try to get Frankie's attention, it dawns on her that he's that dangerous, secret kind of handsome that sneaks up on you. At first, he feels like an average anybody, but there's an energy about him, a crook in his confidence that makes you want to dive headfirst into his chest. Or, in Frankie's case, flap your lips without saying a word while fingering a head of lettuce.

Jules takes pity on both the lettuce and Frankie and separates them while answering for her sputtering brother. "He spends all day on his knees at Murphy Industrial."

Hugo laughs but doesn't take his eyes off Frankie, who huffs his indignation toward Jules and moves away to remove a tablecloth from the back table. The market is wrapping up, so Frankie busies himself with breaking things down. Hugo looks to Jules again as if to ask permission. When she nods, Hugo slips into the booth to help Frankie with the tablecloth, which is more troublesome than it would seem. Jules watches Frankie start to say he doesn't need help but stops, and something in his quiet resolve makes Jules unexpectedly tear up. A softness returns to her brother that he has kept tucked away for the last few months. As they fold the tablecloth together, it forces them to close the gap between them, and Jules watches her brother fight and welcome the dance. The way Hugo watches him, unable to make eye contact, while still moving closer is undeniably sweet, like a patient child coaxing a scared, hissing kitten out of a corner. When they are less than a foot apart, Frankie glances up at Hugo but pulls the tablecloth away from him, making the last few folds himself.

Jules is tempted to turn away and give them some privacy, but how can she when Hugo says, "Wow, first we bonded over plastic curtains, now it's plastic tablecloths. What's next, plastic sheets?"

Jules howls with the kind of unbridled laughter that sends the birds racing from the nearby tree, and at least one baby nearby bursts into tears. Frankie is less entertained and throws the tablecloth on a stack of vegetable crates and then lifts the stack before heading off toward their father's truck.

Jules watches Hugo watch him go. With his head tipped and his brow curled in confusion, he resembles a puppy trying to figure out an animatronic platypus. *Do I hump it or kill it?*

After a moment, he shakes off whatever he's thinking and nods toward Jules. "Well, that was something."

"That it was," she says as he leaves to join a friend who waits across the street with ice cream. Hugo takes the cone from him, and the first lick results in the entire cone crumbling and leaving a trail of ice cream down his shirt as it rolls to a plop at Hugo's feet.

Something about it, on the heels of what she witnessed between him and her brother, feels filthy, and she mutters to herself. "Wow, strong tongue."

She watches Hugo clean himself up the best he can while also glancing back in the direction Frankie had gone. Twice.

"Who was that guy?" Clayton asks, nodding in Hugo's direction as he slides the vegetable bins out from under the table.

"With any luck," Jules says, patting her dad on the back. "That's your next son-in-law."

He has no response to that, so she locks up the portable safe and takes it and anything else she can carry to her dad's truck. She spots Frankie standing off to the side under a tree near the parking garage, his arms crossed and deep in thought, staring into the darkness of a nearby alleyway. She watches him for a moment, the noise of his unsettled mind adding to the cacophony of the market shutting down around her. He takes a deep breath that he holds for a beat, closing his eyes and exhaling slowly. He must sense her watching because he glances toward her with a forced smile that shifts as he looks away again, now in the direction Hugo had gone. She doesn't know what happened there, but she chooses to believe it represents the start of something good.

Her phone buzzes, and she hops up to sit on the open bed of her dad's truck to check her messages. She missed a text earlier from Damon saying he was taking Sophie to lunch with his mother. The messages coming in now are from Joshua, a series of short texts that vibrate her fingers.

Recording at SoundFarm.

Wanna visit?

No pressure.

Okay, some pressure.

Your call.

But come.

It's hard to decide which of the four thousand voices in her head she should let respond, so she decides against all of them and tucks her phone away instead. She hops down from the truck and heads back to help her dad clear away the last of this week's market. She glances back toward where Frankie had been standing.

He's gone.

This immediately undoes all the softness she was starting to feel for him because it means he's left her to finish up the market, even though she specifically told him she wasn't doing it this time. She stomps back to their booth, ready to tattle to Daddy like they're back in grade school, but she finds Frankie sweeping up the vegetable remains that are the sacrifice of market chaos as JP holds the dustpan for him. He glances back at her.

"I said I'd be here," he says. "You are free to go find some trouble." He says it like he knows her secrets, and he probably does.

"Thanks," she says, and she pulls out her phone. As she walks toward her truck, she looks back to Frankie as if asking permission, but he's distracted with his tasks at hand, so she's left to her own devices.

She bites her lip so hard that she tastes the hint of blood and then texts back to Joshua.

Maybe.

18

VERTIGO.

IN DOWNTOWN DES MOINES, there are magic tunnels in the sky. Frankie has always appreciated the downtown skywalk system. Stretching 4.2 miles and connecting 55 buildings, it allows people to get around while protected from extreme weather, whether rain, snow, sleet, or, like today, humidity. It's not lost on him that this sometimes means walking an extra half-mile just to avoid going outside and walking across the street, but Frankie's not built to care about such things.

After packing out the farmers' market, he skipped returning to his car straightaway, instead going for a walk and finding himself here, standing in the middle of the skywalk overlooking Grand Avenue, leaning his head against the window to look down through the glass lip at the street below. The skywalk is air-conditioned, but he can feel the outdoor heat through his forehead. The external extremes help calm his internal screams. He can sense that people are walking by, but his eyes are closed, so he won't see them. There are giggles and whispers, babies crying, dogs with sudden barks, and muffled street noise. It's overwhelming in the best possible way.

"Have you ever been to the Grand Canyon Skywalk?"

Frankie doesn't need to open his eyes or look up to see who's talking. "Hugo," he whispers to himself. It's the first time he's felt the name on his lips, and it itches, forcing him to scratch his tongue between his teeth.

Hugo carries on the one-sided conversation, ignoring Frankie's silence. "I'm afraid of heights, but when things reach a certain height, my fear vanishes. Can't explain it. I can jump out of a plane, but standing on the balcony over there?" Frankie doesn't look up but imagines he's pointing toward the condos climbing into the sky across the way with shallow outdoor balconies. "Blinding vertigo. The Grand Canyon Skywalk causes me extraordinary terror, but it's worth it. Sometimes, the fear is the reason, right?"

He pauses, and Frankie turns his head just enough to see Hugo's shoes. Red Vans, no socks. Frankie refused to see him too clearly at the farmers' market earlier, much like he tried to hold him as a fuzzy blur when they first met at Shane's house this morning. But now he's taking in the details. Hugo is wearing jeans cut off below the knee that reveal thick, defined calves and a pale yellow T-shirt emblazoned with something in red that Frankie can't see. This shirt doesn't ring a bell with what he had on earlier, but why would he change in the last half hour? Beyond that, what he also notices about the shirt is how it reveals that Hugo's stomach has a bit of a paunch as he breathes. It makes his rugged handsomeness less intimidating to know that there aren't abs of steel to contend with also, not that Frankie is thinking about contending with anything Hugo might have to offer.

Hugo's back is to the window, and he's propped against the railing. His hands are hanging loose, and he's wearing a thick sports watch with the face turned to the wrist side. The muscles in his forearm pulse a couple of times, sending an electrical jolt to Frankie's zipper.

Frankie closes his eyes momentarily and counts to three to ward off an erection. "I'm sorry about this morning."

"It's okay. You're allowed your madness. You've had a rough couple of months."

"How do you know what my last few months have been like?"

Frankie turns to find that Hugo is now holding the banister and squatting down low, probably stretching something that only boys like him would stretch. *Show-off,* Frankie decides, and it almost alleviates the desire to touch the tease of flesh that is peeking out between Hugo's T-shirt and shorts. His eyes move up to find Hugo looking up at him over the broad shelf of his upper arm. He can't see his mouth (thank God) but can tell he's smiling. Frankie wonders if it's possible to stop a blush before it happens, even as he feels his cheeks flush.

"It's the smallest big city," Hugo says as he stands, reaching over to pick something off Frankie's shirt, or he would have if Frankie hadn't swatted him away. Hugo acknowledges the move with his eyes but not his mouth. "And you own one of the few gay hangouts. How many secrets do you think you have?"

"Plenty," Frankie answers.

"Don't count on it." Hugo sighs with a look somewhere between impatience and pity. He continues. "What are you doing the rest of the day?"

Frankie offers a single abrupt guffaw as an answer and worries that it will come off as arrogance rather than a pathetic lack of self-esteem.

Hugo waits quizzically, not understanding the response, so Frankie must resort to words again. "Tonight is open mic night at Fuel Injector," he finally says. "I should be there."

"That starts at, what, eight?"

"Why are you asking?" Frankie asks with growing frustration, and Hugo smiles with that goddamn beautiful mouth.

"So that means you're free for the next …" he pauses to glance at his watch, and Frankie refuses to notice how thick his wrists are. "Five hours?"

Why is Frankie nodding, and what the hell is going on?

"I have a suggestion," Hugo says and then lets the silence fill in the blanks.

Frankie gives up, asking, "Are you going to give it to me?"

He feels his cheeks erupt in flames as he imagines the hundreds of offensive and graphic ways Jules would respond to his question. Hugo takes the bait and leers, "Do you want me to give it to you?"

The game suddenly feels tiresome, and Frankie just wants to go home and eat a bag of feelings. He starts to leave but Hugo grabs his arm and turns him back. Frankie yanks his arm away and immediately regrets it. *Sorry, please, touch me again. Here and here and here and definitely here.*

"Sorry," Hugo apologizes. "That was borderline offensive. I just wondered if you might listen to me with an open mind."

Frankie wants to understand, but he's also distracted by Hugo's T-shirt. At first glance, it reads "I (heart) OTK," but the heart is upside down. Hugo sees Frankie staring at his chest and looks down. "Oh shit. This stupid shirt. It's Andrew's. I spilled ice cream down my front earlier. This was in his trunk."

"What does it mean?"

Now it's Hugo's turn to spin in discomfort. "How about this? You answer my question first, and then I'll tell you about the shirt?"

"What if I say no?"

Hugo gives a sexy smirk that allows him the upper hand for now, if not for all time. "Then I'm not going to tell you what my shirt means."

Frankie lets the silence return, and this time, Hugo relents and says, "Okay, look, you seem like a lone wolf. I respect it. I do. But maybe you should run with the pack today."

He pauses, perhaps worried about how ridiculous his suggestion is, but then plows ahead. "Friends of mine are getting married this afternoon, and I want you to come with me."

The suggestion is so unbelievably absurd that Frankie's only sane response is to walk away, which he does. For seven months he ignored every invitation except those his family had guilted him into. He doesn't even go to a movie with his friends, and that only involves sitting in the dark for two hours, not talking to people he'd actually want to talk to under different circumstances. A *wedding?* This guy is crazy.

Hugo trails him. "I know it sounds crazy, but I thought maybe you'd want to get out and see people. People would love to see you. It could be good for you."

Frankie doesn't even turn around. "Suddenly, you know what's good for me? You don't know a thing about me." Frankie spits the words and has to wipe his mouth. "Just stop."

Hugo freezes, but his words continue to chase Frankie. "You stop."

Confused, Frankie turns back. "Stop what? I'm not doing anything."

"Exactly," Hugo says. "Stop not doing anything. DO SOMETHING. Life isn't gonna wait for you to be ready."

Frankie stomps toward him, hoping to scare Hugo, but Hugo stands his ground. "Why are you doing this?" Frankie asks. "This morning was humiliating enough, and now I can't get rid of you. Did I suddenly become a project for you, like some stray dog you found? Leave me alone."

Hugo locks his jaw. "Make me."

Frankie suddenly understands The Hulk more than he ever has. The rage that races through his veins threatens to shred his skin. "'Make me'? What are you, nine?"

"Twenty-nine," Hugo says.

"Jesus," Frankie says. "You're a goddamn baby. No wonder you don't understand."

"But I'd like to," Hugo says, and Frankie is taken aback by the sincerity in his voice and eyes. "What are you scared of?"

Inside Frankie, words are jackhammering the back of his teeth, and he wonders what it would feel like to let it all spill out, to finally let go of this rage and doubt and pain. But if you start, how do you stop?

"I'm not scared, Hugo," he says, tiptoeing around the truth. "I'm tired. I don't know what this is, what you're doing or wanting, but I'm not interested. Not that it's what you're suggesting, but the idea of dating? Having sex? Trusting someone? I can't. Maybe someday, but certainly not today. So, please, just leave me alone."

Exhausted, Frankie turns back to lean his head against the window again, resuming the position where Hugo had found him, partially hoping that he'll open his eyes and see that the last few minutes have all been a weird daydream.

Hugo shatters that wish with a heavy sigh as he copies Frankie and leans his head against the glass.

"Shane is a piece of shit," Hugo says. He then glances at Frankie, maybe waiting for permission to say more. Frankie glances at him with only the smallest of shrugs, so Hugo continues. "I knew Shane. I'm not one of his notches, but my ex is. Another goddamn prize. He said he was going to the gym one day, but I didn't believe him, so I followed him. He ended up at Shane's house, your house. When I texted him to come outside, things ended in your front yard while Shane watched from the window. We'd been together for 10 years. I met him when I was 19 and had been disowned by my parents. He convinced his parents that I cheated on him, so then my second family disowned me. Infidelity is a grenade, not a bullet. It blows up everything around you. That's the hardest thing to learn."

Frankie feels a shift that resembles camaraderie. For the first time in seven months, the silence isn't treated like a weapon but a truce. It relaxes places in Frankie's body he hadn't even realized were clenched. He sighs, heaving against the window, and almost smiles at the sensations tickling his toes, jaw, and lower back.

He glances over to see Hugo smiling even as he's facing away. "You're considering being my date to the wedding, aren't you?"

Frankie doesn't have the strength to pretend. As an answer, Frankie grins and asks, "So, what does your T-shirt mean?"

Hugo does a tiny victory dance that is the cutest goddamn thing Frankie has ever seen.

"OTK stands for 'over the knee,' " Hugo says as he circles back to Frankie. "It's a spanking fetish. It's a joke … and it's Andrew's shirt."

Frankie responds with a shake of his head. "I'm not sure how much of that is true."

"Only one way to find out," Hugo says, pulling Frankie away from the window. "Let's go."

19

UNICORNS.

THERE'S A SECTION OF Des Moines that, not so long ago, no one wanted to be caught dead in unless they were, well, dead. But then buildings in this area started to be purchased and renovated, and the area started coming back to life. "Back to life" implies that this area ever had a life, which is both true and false. The warehouses between the Capitol building and downtown housed mechanics, industrial tools, and overflow paperwork from the various state departments. Not exactly a place the cool kids wanted to hang out. That changed several years ago, and now it's vibrant and growing.

Frankie used to saythat the gays saved this city, just like they've saved all the rest. He meant it as a joke, but Clayton had come to learn that it was also a truth. When Frankie finally said the words out loud, "I'm gay," both Clayton and Carol were not surprised but also terrified and confused. It didn't make sense to Clayton. To Carol, either, but she seemed to have an easier time settling into it as a fact of life. Clayton struggled, and still does, to understand it. He talked to Pete about it for a long time. They shared crude jokes and open-hearted confusion, but then Pete asked, "Do you think you could fake it?"

The question seemed like the setup for a joke, and Clayton tried to play along. "Depends on what you're asking me to do?"

They laughed about it for a moment, but then Pete got serious. Pete was rarely serious, so when he was, it demanded attention. "Think about it. If I told you, for whatever reason, you were required to be gay for a day, could you do it? Not the actions. Not the sex part because, really, I don't want to think about logistics. But the love part. You have to love a man with the same kind of passionate desire you have loved any woman. Could you force yourself to make that feeling real?"

Clayton prepared a snide comeback, but then he let the question really sink in. Pete had bravely asked him a real question, and, respectfully, that required a real answer. "No, I could not."

Pete raised his hands as if to clarify this was all that needed to be understood. "Well, then. That's your answer. Frankie feels what he feels, and anything else is an impossible lie to tell. I'd imagine he has tried to force a different truth, and it's quite possible that the struggle has nearly killed him, based on the pills and the depression and the trouble. We both know it has killed plenty of children. Plenty of people. Love your kid. That's your only job."

For a man who didn't seem to have a lot to say, Pete could

sure say a lot. In that conversation, Clayton settled into the truth of what it meant to love Frankie as if it was within his power to stop loving him. In the years since Frankie's coming out, he has witnessed and read about parents turning their backs on gay sons and daughters. While coming to terms with Frankie's truth was a challenge, the idea of turning his back on his flesh and blood was never an option. He couldn't let go of either of his children any easier than he could let go of his own heart.

Clayton remembers this conversation with Pete as he drives through the warehouse district, officially renamed the East Village several years ago. He had been tricked into attending his first Gay Pride parade on this very street a decade ago. Carol claimed she needed something from the kitchen supply store, so he drove her—willingly, but warily—into the warehouse district. Carol claimed to be just as surprised as he was to find the streets shut down, rainbow flags everywhere, and a drag queen on stilts waving at children. "Oh my," Carol said, feigning surprise. "Well, since we're here … ." He tried to protest, but she squeezed his hand in a way that said *we're doing this*, and she didn't let go for the next hour. Once he go over the shock and, admittedly, some confusion, Clayton found it all eye-opening, to say the least.

He had never seen so much joy worn so loudly. It was chaotic, colorful, unapologetic—and entirely foreign to a man raised on stoicism and church potlucks. But in the middle of all that noise, he found himself watching the way people looked at each other. Not just the couples, but the kids in glitter, the moms holding homemade signs, the old men crying from joy and camaraderie on benches.

Frankie came out when he was twenty-four, but it was as if he said the words and then went back in the closet, at least as far as his parents were concerned. He didn't talk about that part of this life. There were no introductions to new friends with any kind of indication that any of them were anything more than actual friends. It eventually reached the point where Clayton and Carol were guessing which of Frankie's friends could be a romantic match for their son. Carol had her fingers crossed for Daron Schatz, a nursing student and one of Frankie's roommates after college. Clayton wasn't such a fan of Daron's, instead rooting for Markus Brenton, an attorney and a farmer's son. Frankie had brought him around several times. And Markus was a huge football fan, a gene Jules had acquired instead of Frankie.

Clayton was surprised to find a gay man that liked sports. Until this new chapter opened up, Frankie was his only perception of what it meant to be gay, so he assumed Frankie defined homosexuality. A ridiculous concept, of course, but a reality that Clayton had to learn to move around. And Markus helped him do that as much as Frankie did. They were opposites in a way that seemed to draw them together, and Clayton saw Frankie happier around Markus than he had ever seen his melancholy son before. They whispered and joked and shared private glances that had meanings that only they understood.

So, when Daron Schatz and Markus Brenton got engaged a year later, Clayton was devastated. He assumed Frankie was as well and got up the gumption to discuss it one night with his son.

"Oh my God! Markus?!" Frankie howled when Clayton finally revealed that he thought Frankie and Markus would end up together. It was a conversation overflowing with discomfort as Frankie's love life had never been discussed, at least not since he'd taken Missy Vargus to the junior prom.

Frankie was pale with discomfort at trying to ease his father's disappointment over this lost romance. "I will spare you the grotesque details, but trust me when I tell you that is the absolute worst idea. We would kill each other. Meaning I would kill him. I love him like a brother, but he's insane."

Jules had overheard the conversation and had to pipe in. "Wait, isn't Markus Brenton the one with the fish story?"

Frankie turned beet-red and struggled for words as he pulled Jules away from Clayton, whispering, "Don't ever repeat those words in this house again."

Clayton didn't know what that meant, and he was sure he didn't want to know, especially after hearing Jules's vicious laughter in the next room. At dinner that night, when the meal happened to include fish, Clayton tried not to notice Jules ate it in a way that made Frankie laugh beer out his nose.

Though the conversation about Markus was rich with uneasiness, it also shifted Frankie's comfort level, reassuring him that he was safe to bring home friends who were more than friends. Shortly after, Clayton and Carol were introduced to Quinn Yates, a smart young man from one of Frankie's college classes. It was the first time Clayton saw his son hold the hand of another man. It made Clayton unexpectedly uncomfortable and even angry. As they were all sitting in the living room watching "Survivor", he had to leave the room because his peripheral vision saw Frankie and Quinn's fingers intertwined on the sofa. He went to the kitchen with the excuse of needing another beer and then pulled on his boots with plans to work in the garden. But Carol stopped him with sharpness in her voice. "Take off those goddamn boots and come watch TV."

He stood looking at her for a long time, one foot in a boot, the other socked foot begging to follow. She came over and hugged him. "I know," she said against his cheek. "But this is what it is. This is what love is."

She left him to his own decision, and he sat alone in the kitchen for a long time. He kept going back to his conversation with Pete. He thought about the first time he had seen Jules hold the hand of a boy. She was 14 and sitting on the porch swing with Tyler Zambrano when Clayton brought out the lemonade Carol had asked him to deliver. They pulled their hands apart when Clayton arrived, but they couldn't have been more obvious. So much rage surged in Clayton that he nearly lost balance as he set the lemonade down, telling Tyler he should head home soon. "She's too young," he had said to Carol later.

"Too young to what?" Carol asked. "Grow up?"

The question made more sense than he wanted it to, and Clayton had to come to terms with the facts. He wanted to protect her, keep her innocent and safe. Isn't that a father's job? Maybe that's what he wanted for Frankie. To keep him safe. And any risk to that threatened Clayton. Frankie being gay confused Clayton because he struggled to make sense of it, but it also scared Clayton because he feared for Frankie's safety.

And that realization inspired him to make margaritas before heading back to watch the season finale of "Survivor."

He noticed Quinn whisper something to Frankie a few minutes later, and Frankie nodded behind his margarita before quickly wiping away a tear and turning his attention to the television. Clayton glanced over at Carol, and she winked at him, adding a subtle toast with her glass. Clayton couldn't control if his son was safe in the world, he told himself, but he could make sure he felt safe in this house. That's the job.

Later that night, he and Carol lay in bed and talked about it for hours. It turned out to be their most intimate conversation. While discussing their fears and doubts and anxieties, they made love in a way that brought them both to tears, a first for Clayton. It didn't feel like sex; it felt like healing.

The next day, they drove to the East Village for lunch and shopping. Carol had insisted on going to a gay bar for an afternoon cocktail, but Clayton declined; he wasn't ready for that. Now he's parked in front of Nowhere Bar with plans to go in by himself in the middle of the day on a Saturday. He's got Mona's grill put together and strapped in the bed of his pickup, but before he drops it off, he catches a glimpse of a store across the street that he remembers Carol taking him to, so he decides to pop in there first.

De Lovely is a sliver of a shop selling soaps, lotions, and a wide variety of tiny bottles and jars full of things Clayton doesn't understand. When he steps into the quiet shop, the first thing he notices is how calm it feels to be there. Carol would probably tell him it was the magic of the chamomile or sage or pixie dust in one of the magic potion bottles, but he guessed it was something else. He has vivid memories of being here with Carol. That's what calms him. He sees her everywhere in the house and around the farm. He remembers being with her at the café with Jules. But this is the first new place in a while that holds old memories, and he closes his eyes to soak in them, hoping maybe when he opens his eyes, he will see Carol sidling up beside him to offend his nostrils with some strange concoction.

He looks around, and he suddenly feels wildly out of place. He picks up the closest bar of soap because it feels like the right thing to do. He smells it and immediately regrets it. Why would someone want to wash themselves with something that smells like something you'd like to wash off?

"Hi."

Startled by the voice, Clayton fumbles with the soap, sending it sliding across the floor to disappear under a display case of candles that probably smell just as–what would Carol call it?--earthy. Or, more frankly, like dirt. He turns to a woman he knows he's supposed to know. He has seen her several times, not just in this shop but at the café as well. "Mr. Parker! How have you been?"

He smiles and blushes. "I'm sorry. I know we've met."

She wipes away his embarrassment with a wave of her hand. "No worries. I'm Jen."

She looks over the table where he had picked up the soap. "Are you looking for something for Jules?"

"No, my wife."

Jen's big smile momentarily falters. It lets Clayton know that she's heard that Carol left. "She's coming back tomorrow," he adds quickly, "and I want a nice gift. It's our anniversary."

With a wide grin, Jen pats Clayton's arm. "That's fantastic news! Where has she been?"

The question throws him off balance, so he turns his attention to a display of soaps. He picks one up but doesn't smell it for fear of not being able to hide his reaction.

"My Carol likes the ocean," he tells her, moving around the display. "And rain. And grapefruit, no sugar. She likes roses, but she doesn't want to smell like them. 'If that was God's intention, he'd have put thorns where my thumbs are.' She said that once. More than once."

He smiles at Jen. "When we first met, she used to love it when I'd wash her hair. I want something to remind her of who we used to be."

Embarrassed at how silly that sounds and how surprised he is to have said it, Clayton turns away from her, but she tucks her arm into his. "I'm sorry if all the scents in here are irritating your eyes," she says gently as a tear makes its way to the edge of his lashes. "But I think we can find something that Mrs. Parker will like."

He smiles and pats Jen on the hand.

Seventy-five dollars and a lot of forced nods and smiles later, he drops a bag of confusion onto the truck seat. He knows Carol will like it, so that's enough. What he would like is a beer, so he heads across the street toward Nowhere Bar.

Looking up at the huge rainbow flag that flaps above the front window, he shakes his head, remembering the trepidation he had the first time he came here with Carol and Frankie. It didn't help that when he entered the front door back then, they were accosted by a gigantic drag queen passing out glow-in-the-dark shots. Clayton had seen drag queens on television, thanks to one of the shows Carol had started watching, but in real life, it was all so … loud.

Opening the door now, Clayton feels less stressed and more in control. He needs a minute to adjust to the dark interior and stands by the front door, rubbing his eyes. He's never been here without Frankie, and he's never been here in the middle of the day. Other than some borderline pornographic artwork on the walls of men in various states of dress and embrace, it could pass for any small-town dive bar. There's a pool table and a jukebox, ratty, stained carpet, and wood paneling on the walls. The long L-shaped bar takes up a good chunk of the space. He remembers another side bar with a dance floor, but that part must not be open during the day, making the bar feel especially small and somewhat intimidating. There's only a handful of guys hanging out. A few women. A couple of uncertain genders, probably using pronouns Clayton is just starting to understand. A small group of friends playing pool, laughing boisterously, and singing along to a Cher classic that even Clayton knows.

"Well, well, well, if it isn't Mr. Clayton Parker."

Mona Falcone is behind the bar, wearing a shimmery gold T-shirt with a black dagger embroidered between her breasts. As she pulls his handshake into a kiss on the cheek, Clayton notices the zebra-striped leggings she's wearing. This is the bar her son, Joey, had owned until he died. A wildly energetic and openly HIV-positive young man, Joey had been one of the pioneers who fought to renovate this neighborhood. He referred to Nowhere Bar as his church, telling people his signature punchline, "God knows it's full of sinners looking to be saved."

Joey died suddenly four years ago. It stemmed from his weakened immune system, but rumors ran the gamut from murder to suicide. Clayton ignored the gossip; all he needed to know was that a friend had lost a child. He had met Mona and her now ex-husband several times over the years. They had been out to the house for dinner, and Clayton and Carol had been invited to private parties at the bar. He hadn't seen her much since the funeral, and now he's seen her twice in two days.

"How are you, Miss Mona?"

She lets out a low, exaggerated moan as she sets a beer in front of him and arches her back. "Ugh, my blood pressure's rising and my tits are falling. And I think these idiots are trying to kill me."

A waif of a boy wearing camouflage pants, a football jersey, and jewel-encrusted stilettos climbs up on the stool next to Clayton and faces Mona.

"Shut up, bitch, you love it."

Mona smiles like she's either going to hug him or kill him. "Thumper, sweetie, you wouldn't know love if it took a dump on your chest."

Thumper squeals in delight and spins on the bar stool, stopping when his knees knock against Clayton's, causing him to splash his beer. Clayton laughs politely as he licks the beer from his thumb and grabs a napkin to clean up the spill. When he looks up, Thumper fixes him with a crooked grin, "What's your story, Daddy? Wanna play pony?"

He taps his knee against Clayton's, obnoxious with false flirtation. Clayton is uncomfortable but entertained. "I'm not gay."

Thumper grunts. "Neither was my last boyfriend."

Mona swats him away. "Go on, now. Leave him alone."

Thumper quickly becomes aggressive, telling Mona, "People don't come here to be left alone." He turns to Clayton. "What are you looking for if it ain't trouble? You can get a beer anywhere. Why here?"

Clayton tips his head toward Mona. "I wanted to check in on a friend."

Thumper rolls his eyes and slides off the bar stool. He starts to walk away but then comes back to get into Clayton's face. "You like checking out the freaks? Bet you're gonna bruise yourself later thinking about these boys, arncha Grandpa?"

Clayton sees the fists clenching in Mona's eyes, but he calms her with a small nod before turning to Thumper. "Will you kindly take one step backward?"

Thumper mimes stepping back but doesn't actually move, and Clayton gives a genuine smile to this tough, fragile child. He places his hand on Thumper's shoulder and gently guides him to take a full step back. "There, thank you."

He turns in his bar stool to face Thumper, whose expression teeters between indignation and fear. "I can't imagine what your life may have been like," Clayton says. "I've only seen what my son has survived, and I dare to say he had it easy."

He motions to the bar. "He came out here before he came out to me. So that's why I come here. I like to give my money to a place where I know kids like him feel safe."

Thumper's façade of cool crumbles as he nods at Clayton. Then he fishes a wad of money out of his pocket, dropping a few bills on the bar as he turns to Mona. "You oughta climb on that, Miss Mona. Someone should. I'm buying his beer."

Mona is dumbfounded. "What? You don't even pay for your own drinks."

Thumper shoots her a double-barreled middle finger. "Dammit, woman, just let me be generous before anybody sees." Mona accepts the money in disbelief as Thumper lifts his glass off the bar. He glances at Clayton but can't quite face him. "Cheers, Daddy. I was starting to think that men like you were unicorns."

Clayton watches Thumper slink off to rejoin his friends at the pool table, stylishly strutting as if this tattered carpet were a Paris runway. He turns to find Mona grinning from ear to ear as she pours herself a shot. "Hell on fire, you're good. I would pay a million bucks to see the look on his face again."

She taps his beer glass with her shot. "To the unicorns."

Clayton taps his bottle to her glass. "To the unicorns."

20

RECIPE.

JULES STARES AT the latest text messages with Joshua.

Maybe yes or maybe no?

Maybe maybe.

Why had she said maybe? She couldn't possibly go see him at SoundFarm. Certainly not today. She was exhausted and grimy from the farmers' market and had been distracted from showering when she got home by the sudden need to find her grandmother's pineapple pie recipe. It was one of her father's favorites and she wanted to sweeten the blow of whatever tomorrow would bring for the family. She hoped to get it made this afternoon before going to the open mic at Fuel Injector.

She tucks her phone into her pocket and returns to her search, pulling down another box from the shelves Damon had installed in the garage. Several of the boxes and bins had labels for Halloween and Christmas decorations, camping gear, and paint supplies, but it was the unmarked boxes that held the collection of photo albums, school art projects, camping and sports gear, and, hopefully, grandma's recipe cards. The box she's pulling down now is surprisingly heavy, revealing itself to be hiding another smaller box on top that slides off as she tips the bigger box. She manages to duck out of the way before being smacked in the face by the runaway box, but it hits her in the shoulder before flipping over her back and splashing its contents all over the garage floor behind her.

She sets the box she's holding on the workbench and turns to survey the mess just as she is startled by the garage door jumping to life, starting its ascent. She clutches her racing heart as the door opens, revealing Damon sitting in his car in the driveway. He gets out and comes over to her. "What are you doing?"

"You scared the shit out of me," she says more accusatorilly than intended. "I'm trying to find my grandma's pineapple pie recipe."

She kneels to rummage through the random assortment. It feels promising as these are all mementos from her grandmother. Damon joins her and flips over a photograph of Jules as a little girl, holding hands between her mother and grandmother and swinging to kick her feet in the air. He hands it to her, and she tucks it into her pocket before collecting a couple of doilies and needlepoint tea towels that had slid under a broken treadmill that hadn't yet found its way to the dump.

"So, Clayton honestly believes she's coming back tomorrow?" Damon asks, and she nods without turning back to him.

"Sad the things we need to believe just to get through the day, huh?"

She nods again, sitting back to exhale as she realizes something. "I'm assuming you know where our daughter is."

"Doing what she's gotta do to find the dollars," he says in a tragic attempt to sound like a gangster. "Girl's late on her rent."

Jules rolls her eyes as she interprets this. "So, she's in your brother's pool?"

"That's what I said," Damon replies, sliding a yellowed index card splattered with time and stains from an old *Better Homes & Garden* magazine. Squinting at the faded, loopy penmanship, he read aloud, "Pineapple dream in coconut crust. … Damn, was your grandma older than the word 'pie?'"

Jules laughed despite herself. "You leave my grandma alone."

She reached out to snatch the card away, but Damon pulled it back, and she fell against him. They wrestled for a minute, giggling and play-fighting. His touch reminded Jules of secrets she had forgotten, and she felt the need to remember everything. They pause briefly, face to face, catching their breath. He recognizes the shift in her and leans forward to gently touch his lips to hers. She welcomes his kiss and shifts to better align with his body. She feels how his groin reacts and, suddenly, they are kissing like two drowning people trying to give each other air. They can't seem to get close, pushing and pulling, accidentally smacking faces and chests as they find their way to the garage floor. His hand moves between her knees and she opens for him, gasping as his thumb brushes over her softest spot. She equally reaches for him, making him growl when she gives him a tug through his shorts. She pushes him onto his back and kisses him so hard that she hears him gasp an "ow," and it only makes her push harder against him until he stops her.

"No, wait," he says, grabbing her wrists to freeze them both with a pained look on his face. "There's something …"

Damon shifts his weight with a groan, sliding Jules off him and sitting up. Reaching around to the ground behind him, he shows Jules the old-fashioned hand-crank eggbeater that she had been wrestling him against. "Apparently, your grandma didn't like my pie joke."

They laugh together like they used to, back when it sounded spontaneous, not just courteous. She wraps her fingers in his and listens closely for the "ting" as their wedding bands tap together. For the first time in a while, she doesn't want to pull away. But she does, with genuine regret. There were things to be done, and she is behind schedule.

"We could take this to the safety of our bed," he says, standing up and revealing that at least part of him was very much interested in continuing that particular kind of conversation. She lets him pull her up to stand beside him, and when they kiss again, he knows that the moment has passed.

"Sorry," she says. "I've got a lot to do."

"But we've got the house to ourselves for a couple of hours," he says, pouting and pulling her into a hug, resting his chin on top of her head.

She wraps her arms around him and closes her eyes against his chest. When she steps back, he has accepted the reality of what is and isn't going to happen. He gives her a quick kiss and reaches down to grab the recipe card again.

"Make the pie," he tells her. "I'll clean up this mess."

She thanks him and heads to the house, where she is happy to discover that she has all the ingredients for her grandmother's recipe. It comes together relatively quickly, with the hope that she correctly interpreted "just enough salt" and "a smidge of vinegar." While the pie baked, she took a shower and went about deciding what she was going to wear to open mic night. For some reason, nothing she pulled out felt right. She was sitting on the bed staring blankly into her closet when Damon came in.

"I know that look," he says, and she blushes because she is also holding her phone with the latest message from Joshua.

How's that maybe feeling now?

"What look?" she asks, slipping her phone under her thigh.

"It's a look of guilt," he says, and she literally chokes a bit, covering it with a cough to clear her throat until he continues. "If you want to go buy something new to wear tonight, go ahead."

"Maybe I will," she says, as if it's a confrontation.

He seems confused by her tone and shrugs, leaving the room.

She follows him to the kitchen, where he checks on the pie before turning to find her watching him. "What?"

"I don't need to buy something new for tonight."

He looks at her blankly. "Are you trying to convince me or yourself?"

She's confused by the irritation growing inside her. "Why

would I need to buy something new? It's just the stupid open mic night."

Damon realizes he's accidentally stepped into a trap he doesn't know how to escape. "I don't know. If you invited Joshua, maybe…"

"I didn't invite him!" she shouts louder than expected. "And even if I did, why would that make me want to buy a new outfit?"

Damon's tone matches hers. "I'm not suggesting you should. Go buy something, or don't. I don't care. Either way, you should probably put on more than that."

He motions toward her, and as she follows his gaze, she realizes she's standing in the middle of the living room in nothing but her favorite, slightly worn, sexy underwear, her bra dangling loosely from one hand. She's caught off guard for a moment, seeing herself fully in this state for the first time in what feels like ages. Her skin feels shockingly disconnected from the body she remembers, and she's lost in the surprise and awe of her own flesh.

She runs her hand over the map of her life, tracing the stories etched into her body by time—the low C-section scar on an abdomen that is now soft where it was once firm, the small, faded marks from where her gallbladder was removed. Her fingers linger on the silvery lines of stretch marks that weave across her thighs, stomach, and breasts. There's a scratch on her hip, maybe from rolling around with Damon earlier, or possibly it happened at the farmers' market this morning.

"This is who I am now," she says to herself, taking it all in. There's sadness here but also pride and acceptance. She looks up at a bewildered Damon, briefly forgetting he was there. She smiles at him just as the timer dings, letting her know the pie is done.

It also confirms at least one other decision.

"You're right," she tells Damon. "I think I will buy something new. No more maybes."

21

RECEPTION.

THINGS HAVE BEEN a blur since Hugo dragged Frankie out of the skywalk. They got a drive-thru lunch and ate in the car while driving to rummage through a consignment shop for attire befitting a gay garden wedding. Hugo had pushed on Frankie a floral shirt with a wide collar to be paired with plaid pants. Frankie was surprised to find himself considering it but decided he wasn't quite ready for "all that." Instead, he settled on a pink dress shirt with paisley cuffs untucked over cotton seersucker chinos. Hugo pouted for a bit but then chose the floral shirt for himself to go with a pair of plum-colored trousers he had in his trunk, because why wouldn't he?

And now they're standing side by side in an immaculately designed courtyard garden tucked behind a corner lot Victorian home that had been converted from a residence to a restaurant on the first floor and living quarters above.

There's a small neighborhood near downtown where the blocks are lined with turn-of-the-century Victorian homes that used to house the city's upper echelon before falling into dilapidation, only to be saved, salvaged, and gentrified by the gays and artists in the early 80s. Now, it's known for gorgeous homes, small cafes, beautiful gardens, and one award-winning restaurant, which is where Frankie somehow finds himself.

Frankie had occasionally been here for dinner but had never seen the backyard. It was a lovely oasis perfect for events like this: a quaint gay wedding with maybe 50 people in attendance. It was an informal affair with the grooms-to-be mingling with the guests before the ceremony, both dressed in fitted silver gray suits with a single blood red rose on the lapel to match their ties; one in a classic pinstripe necktie of red, gray, and white, the other's a matching print but tied in a bowtie. Both grooms are named Brian, though one spells his name "Bryan." Frankie recognized them both and suddenly realized he may have once made out with "Bryan with a y" in the corner of a bar many years ago. Brian is less friendly to Frankie than Bryan is when the couple swings by while making their rounds. Bryan is quick to give Frankie a hug, while Brian can only manage the kind of smile an executioner might give before pulling the lever.

"Well, holy hell, Frankie Parker!" Bryan howls into Frankie's ear mid-hug. "I have not seen you in ages, ya filthy bitch. How are you?"

Brian manages a flat "hi" before looking away in search of someone worthy of his attention. But his soon-to-be husband is gripping his hand, keeping him handcuffed to his side.

"Can you believe I'm getting married?" Bryan nearly sings.

Frankie fights the temptation to answer honestly, settling for "I'm happy for you."

Bryan gets teary-eyed and glances over at Brian. "I didn't expect it, but it's been the loveliest surprise."

Frankie interprets Brian's glance at him as a smirk, as if to say, "Haha, I got him, and you suck." He wonders if Brian knows about Frankie's make-out session with Bryan. If he does, so what? It was before they were a couple. ... Wait, it was from before they were a couple, wasn't it? Wait again. Did either or both of them sleep with Shane? Frankie winces at the fresh memory of Shane, and it quickly turns to paranoia as he glances around, wondering how many of the men here were part of Shane's sexual tour of the city.

Brian pulls Bryan away just as Andrew approaches Frankie and Hugo. Frankie and Andrew were closer friends 15 years ago, pre-Shane, when Frankie was young and dumb instead of old and dumb. They hung in the same circles and had a good time together but never really clicked one-on-one. They had little to talk about unless there was a third to lead the conversation. He had noticed Andrew with Hugo at the farmers' market, but it somehow skipped clicking into place that this was the Andrew who had the spanking T-shirt in his car. If memory serves, that makes sense.

Andrew pats Frankie on the arm with a "Hey, man" and leans in to whisper something to Hugo that clearly isn't great news. Hugo sighs, then turns to Frankie. "Ugh. Can you wait here? I have to deal with someone, and I'm not ready to show you my ugly side."

Before he can stop himself, Frankie says, "I doubt you have an ugly side."

Hugo winks at him. "Good answer. You gonna be okay?"

A bartender passes by with a tray of mimosas, and Frankie grabs two. He holds them up with a smile. "Yeah, I'll be fine."

Once Andrew and Hugo disappear into the crowd, Frankie feels like an idiot holding two drinks and looks for a place to sit one down. There are a couple of stand-up tables around the courtyard, but small groups of chatty people surround them, and his energy level is draining fast. It's been so long since he's been social that he's forgotten how exhausting it can be. It feels like running a marathon after waking from a coma.

On the hunt for a bit of privacy, he circles to the front of the house, where the wraparound porch is set with tables for the post-service dinner. No one is out here yet, giving Frankie a break from people. He sips one of the mimosas, which turns out to be straight bourbon in a champagne flute, and he chokes a bit, spilling a bit of both.

"One of those for me?"

Frankie turns to a shockingly handsome man in a loud Hawaiian-print shirt and pink slim-cut Capri pants revealing a calf tattoo of a broken record spilling into an hourglass. He blinks a couple of times, and recognition suddenly clicks into place.

"Bobby?" Seeing his boss out of his shades-of-beige wardrobe and in the daylight feels unnatural. It suddenly dawns on him that all the confusing discomfort he'd been feeling in the file room was good old-fashioned sexual tension. *Shit, Jules was right.* He hands Bobby one of the glasses. "Beware, it's not a mimosa."

Bobby laughs. "The Brians aren't classy enough for mimosas."

Frankie can only stare at him for a moment, dumbfounded. "Wow. My gaydar sucks."

Bobby laughs and taps his glass against Frankie's. "Cheers to that. You really didn't know?"

"I guess I hadn't thought about it."

"Well, that's disappointing," Bobby says with a wink, sipping his drink. He looks around the yard, and Frankie can only stare at him openly. Wait, was Jules right about Bobby flirting? *Dammit.* What is happening?

Bobby glances back toward the party and then brings his mischievous eyes back to Frankie. "It's nice to see you out," he says. "I must say, you jump in with both feet. Brave choice."

Frankie sighs in agreement. "Why go to just any ol' party when you can crash a gay wedding? What's the emotional risk in that?"

"True, true," Bobby says, squinting as the sun intensifies. "But I'm not talking about the wedding. Though I guess you'd have to cross state lines to find someone that Shane hadn't slept with."

The comment is true but also cruel and confusing. "What does that mean?"

"I mean, Hugo and Shane…" Bobby's demeanor collapses into pity as what Frankie assumes is his expression based on the burning in his cheeks. "Oh, shit. I assumed you knew."

Frankie feels the rage clench his jaw. His ears begin to ring, and his knees turn to mush. He's suddenly dizzy, and Bobby reaches out and steadies him with a strong hand. "I'm sorry to upset you. I just don't want to see you get hurt."

"It's okay," Frankie says, not even trying to sound sincere.

"Shit," Bobby says. "Let me get some water."

"You don't need to," Frankie says to the space vacated by his boss.

To fight nausea, Frankie drops his drink and puts his hands on his knees, leaning forward to catch his breath.

"Frankie?" He doesn't raise his head, just stares at Hugo's red shoes. "Are you okay? The service is about to start."

In response, Frankie lurches down the hill toward the sidewalk. He needs to get away immediately.

Hugo runs after him. "Wait, what's going on? Talk to me."

Raging but not wanting to make a scene, Frankie says, "You slept with Shane, didn't you?"

Hugo stops in his tracks. "What? No. I told you…"

Frankie cuts him off but still can't look at him. "I don't care what you told me. Everybody lies."

He tries to walk away, but Hugo grabs his arm. "Wait, listen to me."

More enraged, Frankie knocks Hugo away, sending him stumbling back into the yard. "If you touch me again, I will kill you."

Hugo stands and brushes himself off. He keeps his distance but also seems to be leaning forward. "Frankie, please. I—"

He raises his hands to reach for Frankie, and Frankie feels the snarl on his lip like a cornered rabid pit bull. The frenzy coursing through his skin scares even him, and Hugo's look shows he's feeling it, too. Hugo's eyes get wide and teary, but he raises his hands in surrender. Andrew comes out onto the front yard, shouting to them, "It's starting."

Frankie glares at Hugo. Hugo starts to speak, but Frankie's expression shuts him down. Instead, Hugo carefully lowers his hands and walks away to join Andrew.

Frankie watches him go, hating that he wants to follow, then forces himself in the opposite direction.

He walks up and down several blocks, lost in his own stupidity. He runs through all the lies of his life that he has ever believed. When his orgy of self-hate exhausts itself, Frankie numbly looks up. He finds he has walked to the apartment building a few blocks over, where he first let himself love a boy.

He was 17, and Elliot Masterson was 18. Elliot wasn't the most beautiful boy, with his buck teeth and angular features, but he was funny and kind. He had the build that Frankie always noticed, thick like a wrestler, dark chest hair peeking out from his polo. Elliot lived in an apartment on the second floor right here with his mother, Dottie. The two first met while working together to build sets at the Des Moines Playhouse. Frankie was terrified when he realized Elliot's touch was more than a friendly handshake. He had invited Frankie over to watch a movie one night when his mom was working her second job at the Perkins by the freeway. Frankie remembers Ethan Hawke was in the movie, but he was more fascinated by the way the TV's blue light played across the features on Elliot's face whenever Frankie snuck looks at him.

Frankie recalled how Elliot had the popcorn bowl balanced on his belly in bed. Frankie laid as far away as possible without falling off. When he was brave enough to reach for the popcorn, he knew part of his mind was actually reaching for the trace of hair between Elliot's shirt and the top of his jeans.

When the movie ended, they lay side by side on the bed until the credits ended and the room fell quiet. The silence was sexy and scary, and Frankie felt his racing heart banging like a drum. He watched Elliot study the ceiling; then he turned to face Frankie. Elliot looked at him silently for a long time, his eyes shifting from exclamation points to question marks. And then he slid his hand across the bed and wrapped his fingers in Frankie's.

"Hi."

They met in the middle to kiss, slowly, awkwardly, over their interlocked fingers. They would meet in the middle a lot over the next few months as they learned about love together. Elliot had been with one other guy "to get it over with," he explained, but this was all new to Frankie. It lasted all summer, and they both seemed to believe the lie that it would survive Elliot going to college two hours away and Frankie's senior year of high school. The lie only held until that first Thanksgiving when Elliot returned, and they realized the shift that could happen between two people. They cried together and promised to stay friends.

Frankie laughed to himself as he realized that was another promise broken. They hadn't seen each other since.

And now Frankie is standing in front of where it all started. He can close his eyes and remember every detail of this place. His mind's eye walks him through the front door, up the stairs to the second floor, through the heavy door to the apartment with the high ceilings, hardwood floors, and built-ins. The comfortable secondhand furniture Dottie had found. The swinging door to the kitchen with the black-and-white tile floor. The clawfoot tub in the bathroom. The arched windows in Elliot's bedroom. The entire apartment felt like a secret hideaway for two lost boys, afraid but also somehow fearless.

Frankie sits on the cement steps leading up to the building and digs out his phone, dialing a number he should have deleted. He knows this call is wrong but also inevitable. It also seems appropriate that he's forced to leave a message, "Shane, it's me. I know you're moving. Where are my green chairs?"

He clicks off the phone and stares at the ground for a long time, watching a parade of ants carrying bits of a discarded cinnamon roll to their own hideaway.

He opens his phone again and does an internet search. He finds Elliot Masterson's Facebook profile. His teeth have been fixed and the angles of his face softened with time, but his eyes are the same.

"Hi," Frankie whispers to his old friend as he clicks on the little gray box in the corner.

Add friend.

22

WEENIES.

AS THE BACK DOOR TO THE BAR opens, the sunlight reminds Clayton that it's the middle of the afternoon. He hasn't been in a bar midday in who knows how long, nor felt the way a beer can undercut your balance while the sun is still high in the sky. He hoists the new grill from the previous day's shopping excursion over the lip of the step as Mona follows him out with a plated stack of hot dogs.

"Let's bet on how long it takes before the first queen cracks a joke about hot weenies," she offers, setting the plate on a side table and firing up the grill. Clayton watches her shimmy, quietly talking herself through all the steps. "First we turn this, now this one, then this little button, and presto."

With a small pop, the grill ignites, and Mona looks over her shoulder with the kind of pride usually reserved for prize fighters. Maybe it's the sun or the beer or the music from the bar, but Clayton realizes that his hips are swaying, which is as close to dancing as he's done in years. Carol used to beg him to go dancing. He'd try to soothe her with a little kitchen foxtrot, but it wasn't enough. She wanted to be out in the world. He tries to remember the last time he danced with Carol, but he gets stuck when he remembers the last night they were together.

After they left Carol's birthday party at Fuel Injector, they watched a recording of Wheel of Fortune. Carol had recently discovered how to use the record function on their cable remote and the queue was full of random movies and episodes. They were each having a small nightcap for their own private birthday party. Carol had brought a bottle of port wine back with her from a girls' trip to Sonoma and had poured them each a bit in the miniature glasses she had also purchased on the trip. She assured him that they were the required vessel for proper enjoyment. He didn't think the port was as exceptional as she did, but he certainly wasn't going to tell her so, especially not on her birthday.

"You're gonna spill," she said aloud, rousing him from falling asleep with the demure glass balanced on his knee. Setting the glass on the side table, Carol took his hand and squeezed it several times. "Silly man."

Then, turning back to the TV, she solved the puzzle. "It's 'Game-Winning Touchdown,' you idiot."

She patted Clayton on the knee when it was revealed she was correct and then headed out to tidy the kitchen. Twenty minutes later, they crawled into bed. Twelve hours later, she walked out.

Thankfully, Mona pulls him out of the memory.

"Ya know," she says as she drops hot dogs on the grill.

"After Joe died, I seriously considered selling this place. Why would I want to surround myself with a constant reminder of his life? But back then, I needed it to survive. But now that I'm surviving? Meh."

Mona arranges the hot dogs in neat rows and lowers the lid.

"You thinking about selling now?" he asks.

She looks intensely at Clayton, and he feels like maybe she's counting the creases on his face. Then she continues. "Maybe. I'm thinking about resting. I've had some offers. But if I sell, it will change. It will be gone. And if it's gone, well, then Joey will really be gone."

Her eyes twinkle with the hint of a tear, and she reaches over to wipe a smudge of grease from Clayton's face. He steps back from her touch and sees the sting in Mona's eyes. It all suddenly feels like too much. He feels relaxed, which makes him feel guilty.

"I'm sorry," he stammers. "I should go. I've got a lot to do, and Carol is coming home tomorrow."

Why do so many people look at him like Mona does when he says this? It's exhausting, and he feels a part of himself shutting down.

"Yep," he continues. "Forty-year anniversary. Hard to believe, I know."

New words are trying to find their way to Mona's lips, so it seems best to make off before the conversation gets uncomfortable. He steps toward the door but stops when she speaks.

"Joey killed himself," she blurts out, and he freezes. He turns back to her, feeling himself nod. It feels like something he already knew, like a secret you'd rather not have.

Perhaps not meaning to say what she just said, Mona turns her attention back to the hot dogs on the grill, giving each a quarter-turn. "I know you knew that," she says with a sigh. "Everyone does, I guess. But I've never said it out loud. Not once in four years. Until now. I guess you felt like the right person at the right time. You've always been kind to me, and you were kind to my Joey. Unlike that asshole father of his, so…there. It's said. And it's true. And I hate it."

Clayton doesn't know how to respond, and he's reminded of the few times he attended marriage counseling with Carol. No one knows, and it's no one's business, but they did. Clayton often sat silent while Carol did the talking. The process was weird and invasive and didn't make sense to him. Why did they have to sit in front of a stranger to be able to talk to each other? But, on occasion, Clayton would have something to say, usually just as they were leaving. "I'm fine with doing this, but I don't understand what me not liking your mother's pineapple pie has to do with me not being honest. I'm not the one who said they were going to Branson and somehow ended up in Manhattan." This is what Dr. Piedmont had called "doorknob therapy." The concept never made sense until this exact moment when Clayton found himself with his hand literally on the doorknob while someone he'd spent hours talking to dropped a bombshell on his toes.

Clayton stumbles over words as he tries to conjure the wisdom Dr. Piedmont might impart in a moment when the response shouldn't be half-assed.

"I don't know what to say" comes out because he doesn't, and there's nothing half-ass about the truth.

"That's better than pretending you do," she responds, flip-flip-flipping the grilled meat with a heavy sigh. "I hate hot dogs."

Clayton's brain is screaming that he should say something else, something comforting.

"How late are you working?" is all he can offer. He hates himself for it. Mona deserves better.

She glances at her watch. "Fonda Dix should be showing up any minute, so I'm about done." She drops the lid on the grill and turns back to him, waiting.

Clayton is in uncomfortable territory. How do people do this for a living? How do people do this at all? "Well, it's open mic night at Fuel Injector. I was planning to go for maybe an hour or so. Then I have to go home and get ready for tomorrow."

She watches him momentarily, waiting for more, and shakes her head. "So … is this the part when I assume that's an invitation?"

Before he can answer, the door to the bar opens between them, and Thumper peeks out.

"Line up, girls!" he shouts back inside. "Mona's playing in the alley with hot weenies!"

Clayton watches Mona as she releases a laugh that sounds like it's on the way to a sob.

She pats Clayton on the arm and then leads him back inside. "I accept your maybe invitation."

23

RED.

A RED DRESS IS THE LAST thing Jules should be wearing, but it's too late now. It's not like she slipped on Julia Roberts's red dress from Pretty Woman. It's a summer dress that happens to be a red bandana print. She's still wearing her cowboy hat and boots. There's nothing fancy about the dress at all, though, truth be told, the fact that she bought it 20 minutes ago might indicate her intentions are suspect.

She checks her face in the rearview mirror to confirm she's planning to go through with this. If she's going to drive away, she has to do it right … now. Her hand doesn't move to shift the truck into reverse; instead she clicks off the engine.

She ignores the man watching her from the small patio and looks around the property like she's trying to understand the layout, though she's been here plenty of times. Hell, the owner is one of her good friends. An hour outside of Des Moines in the tiny country town of Jamaica, is a charming old farmhouse surrounded by acres of cornfields and cattle farms. On the other side of a small family garden, you'll find another house, this one more modern, with a walkout basement and a mid-century industrial vibe. You'll find four bedrooms, two bathrooms, a living room and kitchen, plus a state-of-the-art recording studio where a certain breakout country star might be working on a few songs for his next album.

She shouldn't be here. She should leave.

Instead, she gets out of the truck and smiles at the mountain of a man by the door as he steps forward to greet and stop her. "Can I help you?"

She smiles casually as if all of her intentions are pure. "Hey, is Joshua here?"

"Who's asking?" he asks, scanning her over for stalker vibes.

"Jules."

The henchman's face cracks wide open with a smile. "Julie Parker! He said you looked good, and he didn't lie."

It takes a minute for the recognition to register. "Boyd Crawford? Are you kidding me?!"

She jumps in his arms, and he swings her around in a bear hug before setting her down. "I look good? Holy shit. When did you become The Rock?"

He blushes but also flexes. "Oh, you know, I traded bars for barbells after Jinny died."

Boyd Crawford was a high school hellion and Joshua's best friend. He'd had big football dreams that were sidelined by a drug problem. An overdose almost did him in—and killed his fiancé, Jinny, forcing him toface recovery and grief simultaneously. Though they hadn't spoken in years because of Boyd's downward spiral, Joshua was the first face he saw when he woke up in the hospital. Against the advice of his managers, Joshua took a break from touring just as his star was rising to help Boyd. When word got out as to why Joshua was taking a break, he became a social media superstar, releasing live acoustic videos and surprise singles, interacting with his exploding fan base, and speaking publicly about the stigmas surrounding addiction and depression. When his manager said that Boyd's tragedy was a blessing for Joshua's career, the comment got him fired and punched in the face. Boyd got clean and sober and has been Joshua's bodyguard ever since.

Boyd wraps his tree trunk of an arm around her as he leads her inside. "It's so great to see you. Tell Frankie and your dad I said hi, though maybe he still hates me for tipping his tractor into the ravine." Jules laughs at the memory, cringing at how he avoids mentioning her mother. She knows that people don't bring her up because they don't know what to say, but she'd welcome the chance to talk about it since no one else does. But she knows she can't be the one to bring it up.

He introduces her to several people as they make their way through the house portion of the studio before slipping through a door in the living room that leads to the control room. There, she meets the producer and a couple of other band members. The property owner, Melissa, gives her a quick hug before returning to taking behind-the-scenes photos while her boyfriend mans the board. Through a window, she sees Joshua singing in a sound booth. His eyes widen when he sees her.

He finishes the vocal and loops the headphones on the

microphone before slipping into the control room. "Who let in the groupies?"

He flicks Jules's cowboy hat with his finger, and she thumps his chest. "Depends. Who let in the wannabe?"

The room erupts in jeers at Joshua's expense, and he waves them all to calm down. "I'm taking five," he tells a wired young man comparing several spreadsheets against more notes on his phone.

"Make it three," he says without looking up. "We're on a deadline."

Joshua extends his hand to Jules, and she acts like she doesn't see it, turning back to the room as she heads out. "It was great to meet you all."

Joshua leads her through the dimly lit studio to a larger room set up for a full band. He pushes open a side door that leads outside. As they step out, he lights a cigarette, which Jules promptly pulls from his lips and snaps in half.

He laughs. "Do you remember when you lifted a carton of cigarettes from Casey's, wearing only a bikini and my cowboy boots?"

"Do you remember when lung cancer killed your mother?" she says.

He chokes a bit on her frankness. "Damn, I may have to revoke your groupie status."

He approaches her, and she steps back, focusing on the wide-open spaces around them. They're standing on a large, flat cement patio with two picnic tables, a circle of cushioned chairs around a fire pit, and a hammock. Beyond the patio, the yard dips slightly toward a creek that Jules knows runs on the other side of the tall wild grass, then climbs the hill to the gravel road leading to the highway. She can feel Joshua watching her, and it's both welcome and terrifying. Her eyes drift back to the hammock, and she imagines them slipping into its gentle sway and curling up together, safe in the comfort of entangled limbs and daydreams. But there's nothing safe about that idea, or how she's feeling about what brought her here. She feels the intense energy darting between them. She thinks he must feel it too, because neither one can make eye contact. There is a hunger growing in the pit of Jules's stomach. Only one thing can stop it, but she can't let herself do that.

"I'm married," she says, as if it explains everything. Or anything. She still hasn't looked at him but quickly glances his way to see him nodding a bit, considering this as if it was news he didn't already have. She wants him to say the right thing, even if it's the wrong thing. She wants him to help her make sense of all the crazy, stupid things going on in her mind. She wants him to remind her of who she used to be.

Mostly, she just wants him.

"I know," Joshua says quietly.

"Happily," she adds, maybe a little too quickly.

"That I don't know," he says, and she hates him for it because, the fact is, she doesn't either. Isn't she happy? She has to be happy. Before Joshua walked into the café, everything about the safety of her life with Damon and Sophie felt like more than enough. She wasted no time wishing for anything else because she was content. Isn't that what happiness is? We want to think it's exuberance when it's really just waking up without a sense to run. But if that's true, does that mean her mother was unhappy, or simply unsettled? And isn't all of this in response to her mother's leaving? Would she still have all these feelings if Joshua had swung through town while her mother was still here? But she's not here, and he is. And maybe she should take her mother's advice.

"I knew my mother was leaving," she says, to break the tension and show that she is sure of something. "She flat-out told me, and I didn't realize it. Maybe because she said it so casually."

Joshua looks at her, waiting, unsure what this means to the moment they're in.

Jules continues, "She said, 'I've misplaced my life, and I need to find it while it's still of use to me.'"

Joshua's eyes widened, and the brutality of her mother's words hit her differently as they bounce off his expression. The memory was sharp before, but now it stings. "She said those words while standing behind me in line at Palmer's Deli a month before she left. I hoped she would say more, but this little boy nearby threw chocolate pudding in his mother's face, and we were so stunned that we laughed, and it pulled the conversation in a different direction."

"Did you tell your dad? Frankie?"

She shakes her head, and something about the wide-open country air and the proximity to Joshua's hands makes her crumble a bit. She feels her lip tremble as she fights back tears. Seeing this, Joshua steps toward her, but she stops him, turning away. "I need to go."

"But you just got here." He can't hide the pain in his voice, but she forces herself to ignore it. She can't do this. She can't be this.

She feels her armor returning, a feigned apathy that she

has laid over her pretty summer dress. She clears her throat and straightens her spine. "Tonight's open mic night. Can't imagine you have time, but I wanted to mention it." She's trying to play it casual, friendly, safe. "Fair warning: My friend, Heidi, is a major fan. To the point of probably being mentally unstable."

He's not letting her off the hook so easily. "You could have just called, ya know."

Despite her armor, Jules hasn't yet locked away her heart. "No, I couldn't."

She turns to leave, and his fingertip grazes the back of her arm. Her armor pierced, Jules turns back, grabs Joshua's face, and pulls his lips within an inch of hers. But she stops before the inexcusable can start. Still, her whole body is shaking with desire, and her voice quivers as her eyes move from his lips to his eyes. "I used to think I was just like my father," she whispers.

"And now?"

Her eyes return to his lips because his eyes are somehow more dangerous. The corner of his bottom lip is tucked under his teeth, and she can feel the scruff of his unshaven face against the palms of her hands. It would be so easy. So delicious. So wrong. He gasps a little, waking her to the truth of all she's risking. She releases him and steps back.

"You shouldn't smoke." He had been leaning into her so fully that he stumbled to find his balance. He wipes his hands on his jeans as he recovers, moving back into the real world from whatever fantasy they'd been floating together.

"The show starts at eight," she says as she clears her thoughts, preparing to head home, where she belongs.

"I can't promise anything," he says, reaching for her but then thinking better of it and slipping his hands into his back pockets to keep them contained.

She turns away, glancing at the hammock one more time as she goes. She can't look at this man one more moment if she's going to follow through with leaving.

"Nobody can," she says over her shoulder. "Not really."

24

BRIDGES.

BETWEEN THE NOISE of Nowhere Bar and the expected noise of Fuel Injector later, Mona wisely suggested a breather: that she and Clayton first go for a walk around Gray's Lake. It's a small lake on the south side of town where a path wraps around the perimeter. Clayton agreed and arrived first. Sitting in the parking lot, looking out over the small lake, he feels a twinge of guilt, realizing he hadn't thought of Carol once on the drive from Nowhere Bar. But now, as Mona pulls up in her rusty green Buick Regal, Clayton feels Carol's presence in the passenger seat, side-eye judging him.

Mona's car sputters as it stops with a rattle. Clayton slyly watches as she checks her hair in the rearview. As she tries to get out of the car, Mona finds she hasn't unclipped her seatbelt, so her arms and legs flail, snapping her back into the seat. Clayton can't help but laugh out loud. Neither could Mona, her hearty laugh echoing around the parking lot, the sound soothing all the knots in Clayton's shoulders. He likes that this woman doesn't make time for shame.

When she finally untangles herself from the confines of her car, Mona does a little skip to Clayton's truck.

"Can we pretend you didn't see that?" she says, crossing her eyes and making him laugh again.

"I didn't see a thing," he says, climbing out and following as she leads him to the walking path around the lake.

A long bridge extends over one side of the lake, illuminated with multicolored lights. Dusk is just starting to tug the sun below the horizon, the sun struggling to stay up like a child not ready for bed. The cloudy sky is filled with color reflecting off the lake, where a few late kayakers are gliding across the water, heading back toward the boat launch before the sunset curfew. A couple of birds sail just above the water's surface, their wings occasionally skimming the surface as they scan for dinner. Several people are along the path, though far enough apart that it doesn't feel crowded.

A biker dings his bell as he pedals by Mona at the base of the bridge, and Clayton pulls her back. "My hero," she jokes as the biker curses under his breath.

Along the bridge, small, inscribed plaques commemorate donations and dedications. Mona walks slowly, pausing to read each name as they move across the bridge. Clayton notices that she touches each plaque in memoriam, pausing to rub dirt from any that are unclean.

Clayton feels like he's eavesdropping on a private conversation between Mona and the dearly departed, so he turns his attention to the Des Moines skyline in the short distance. Downtown isn't that big. Just a couple of buildings that could be considered skyscrapers extend above the horizon. It looks the same but feels different. "The city has changed so much in the last few years," he murmurs, mostly to himself. "Sometimes I forget to see what it has become instead of what it was."

He feels Mona's hand touch his elbow. "Sorry, did you say something?"

Her touch raises the hairs on the back of his neck. "Nothing important. Just thinking about change."

"That's certainly not unimportant," she sighs and leans against the railing over the broadest part of the lake. A sharp whistle ricochets off the water, and Clayton sees someone standing on the dock across the lake, waving a red light above his head, signaling the need for everyone to get off the water. Carol looks down at a couple frantically paddle-boating back toward the check-in. "You can do it!" she shouts to them, and they holler back a thank you for the encouragement.

Clayton props his arms on the railing beside her, their shirts touching. He realizes, like a scheming schoolboy, that if he turns his wrist to check his watch, his pinky will brush her wrist. But he can't. Instead, he says, "I'll have to bring Carol here. She always mentioned wanting to ride the paddle boats."

She pats his arm. "I'm sure she'd like that." They continue their walk around the lake silently for a long stretch until Clayton finds himself saying, "She's coming back."

Mona responds with her eyes, if not her lips, and Clayton feels called to explain. He hasn't felt the need to justify his thoughts to anyone, but she had been so open about Joey's suicide that Clayton suddenly wonders what such openness might feel like.

"She does this," he says. "The leaving. Every couple of years, she has to find herself someplace new. She says it's because it makes her appreciate all she has when she gets home. That's why I know she's coming back. She always has."

"Do you want me to respond, or do you need me to listen?"

The question takes him by surprise, and he considers the truth of his answer before responding. "Can you just listen for now?"

"For now," she says.

As they walk around the lake, Clayton speaks almost without pause—about Carol and the twists and turns of their marriage, the joys and worries surrounding Frankie and Jules, his growing fears about aging, and the relentless demands of the farm. Even long-buried grievances, like the unresolved argument with his deceased father, surface unexpectedly.

Mona responds sparingly, offering only a gentle "ah," "oh my," or "I see," but each acknowledgment from her seems to draw more out of Clayton. It's as if her quiet presence unlocks a floodgate within him, releasing stories, opinions, and frustrations he hadn't even realized he was holding onto. Where had all these buried emotions come from? And who was this magical woman to pull so much out of him?

By the time they return to their cars, Clayton is equally energized and exhausted. "Thank you," he tells Mona. "I guess I needed that."

"We all do," she says. "We all need someone to shut up and listen."

"I'm sorry I commandeered a nice walk with my noise," he says, looking back toward the path they had walked.

"Pain isn't noise," she says. "You've got a lot going on. I

hope you threw a few of those worries into the water. Should we go?"

He pauses to make sure he's ready and then nods. "Let's go."

Fifteen minutes later, they arrive at Fuel Injector. Clayton is grateful for their respite at the lake because they walk into a madhouse. The café is buzzing with people, crowding around the bar, shouting orders, toasting, yelling. A man is on the small stage, tweaking a sound system that scratches and screeches as he adjusts a microphone. Without thinking, Clayton takes Mona's hand to lead her through the throngs of people. They dip behind the curtain leading to the small back kitchen, where he finds Frankie unboxing beer bottles with one hand and pouring ice into a bucket with the other.

"Thank God you're here," Frankie says. "Where the hell is Jules?"

Clayton shrugs. He considers mentioning that maybe Frankie now understands how Jules has felt with all the responsibility he has skipped out on recently, but he bites his tongue. When Frankie registers that Clayton is still holding Mona's hand, he lets go sheepishly just as Jules throws back the curtain and darts in. "I'm here! I'm here! Shit! Shit! Shit! I'm sorry!"

Frankie barely has time to glare at her; he's too busy passing beer bottles through a window to the service bar, where Varina hands them to patrons. "I'd ask where you've been, but I bet I know."

He nods toward her red dress as if it explains everything.

Jules is pulling her hair up and tying it back with the twist tie from a loaf of bread. "You don't know anything," she says defiantly, but Clayton senses Frankie knows more than

Clayton wants to hear about.

A shift in the air happens in the café that is strong enough that Clayton pulls back the curtain to see what's happening. A focused hum had fallen over the crowd, which had been chaotic moments before. Whispered excitement tickles the room as people move to allow Joshua to make his way toward where Clayton and Jules are standing. Joshua. He weaves between people, stopping for a handshake, a hello, or a quick hug, followed by a human brick house who looks like an inflated version of one of Jules's jackass high school friends. Clayton isn't in awe of Joshua's star power; he's simply surprised that this kid he once knew as shy with a less-than-promising future would garner such attention.

Jules's friend Heidi stumbles through the curtain, nearly hyperventilating. Clayton wonders if something is seriously wrong with her.

Heidi grabs Jules by the arms to steady herself, "Oh … em … Gee. Is that really my Joshua? He's shorter than I expected. I—I — want to gut him and wear him like a mink."

Jules releases herself from Heidi's death grip and grabs her by the collar. "I need you to pull your shit together, or I will kick your crazy ass out. Got it?"

Heidi nods and backs up, tugging on one of Joshua's concert T-shirts that looks at least three sizes too small. She whimpers and bites her lip, peeking around Clayton to where Joshua has stopped to laugh with Varina. Heidi tries repeatedly to tuck her hair behind her ear, though it's not long enough to stay put, prompting Mona to pull a bobby pin from her hair and clip back Heidi's bangs, who seems oblivious to the assistance.

"My shit is very much not together, but I can do this," Heidi tries to assure Jules seconds before Joshua dips his head under the curtain and brushes against her. "Hey, everyone."

Heidi lets out a choked squeal. Joshua tries to calm her with a smile, only to make it worse. She smiles like a cannibal and blurts out, "I can feel my heartbeat in my vagina."

Joshua's face goes blank as Heidi darts out of the backroom. Clayton watches her weave through the crowd, making a beeline for the front door. Everyone else stands frozen after Heidi's exit until Mona breaks the silence. "Did I imagine that?"

Jules can only shake her head in response, and she and Frankie return to stocking bottles. Clayton watches how Joshua and Jules glance at each other like kids holding a secret but decides to say nothing. He approaches Joshua and shakes his hand. "Hey, Josh. I saw you on one of those award shows. Seeing your mug up there singing with that Sugarland woman was certainly weird."

"Hello, sir," Joshua says, shaking Clayton's hand and nodding a hello to Mona. "If you think it's weird to watch it, you should try being me. It's surreal." Then he turns to Jules. "I don't know how long I can stay."

Jules shrugs him off with a nod as she busies herself. "Whatever."

Joshua dips back into the café, and Clayton watches Jules pretend not to watch him go. He sees flashes of Carol in his daughter that he hadn't noticed before. It's beautiful and painful, and he reaches over to help her stack bottles.

"Good kid, that one," he tells her. "But a wild streak. You're wild enough on your own. That's why Damon is so good for you. You need a rock. You're just like your mother."

At these words, something explodes beneath Jules's surface, and she drops a bottle into the metal sink. It shatters and she looks like she might scream. "I'm nothing like her."

She picks out the broken shards, dumps them into the recycling container, and heads to the café counter. Confused by her outburst, Clayton watches her get lost in the crowd as a guy gets up on stage and takes the microphone.

"Is this on? Good evening, everyone. I'm Tomias Hastings from KFMG. Welcome to another open mic here at Fuel Injector. If you want to perform, your name must be on the list. Of course, we might beg some of you to sing even if you're not on the list."

All eyes fall on Joshua as the crowd cheers. He shrugs, raising his beer in a quiet toast.

"That's not a no," Tomias says as the crowd whoops. He checks a clipboard on the stool next to him. "Okay, first up is Thea Keller."

A waif of a girl with shocking blue bangs and no other hair on her head takes the stage with a guitar that looks to weigh more than she does. Frankie leans against Clayton to say, "I think she's an angry vegan lesbian. Consider yourself warned."

Thea doesn't disappoint as she says with a soft, lispy voice, "Hi. A few weeks ago, I was watching a documentary on ducks. Have you ever seen ducks mate? It's essentially a gang rape. I wrote a song about it called *Trepidation*."

Clayton listens for a few bars and shakes his head, turning to Frankie. "Don't any of these people know any happy songs? I mean, your people commandeered the word gay."

Frankie snorts in agreement and then seems to notice someone in the crowd. Clayton follows his gaze to a young man, whom he recognizes from the farmers' market earlier. Frankie watches the man lean over to whisper to Jules, and she whispers back to him, pointing in the direction where Frankie stands hidden behind Clayton. This guy steps toward them but is stopped by Varina handing him a beer. Clayton looks from the guy to where Frankie is trying to organize a bucket of wine coolers that refuse to cooperate. He shakes the bucket and slams it down on an overturned milk crate.

"I can't do this right now," Frankie says, exiting out the back door.

Clayton stops himself from following Frankie and turns to Mona. "I don't know what's going on with either of my kids."

Mona pats him on the back. "Maybe it's not yours to know."

She glances to the stage as Thea comes to a dramatic, loud, and off-key finish. Mona sighs heavily and reaches for a beer. "That girl needs a steak sandwich."

25

TRUTHS.

OPEN AIR SHOULDN'T feel so claustrophobic. Frankie is in the park behind the café but might as well be stuck in a casket. He rubs his chest as if he can massage away the anxiety clawing at his rib cage. Frankie has been through enough therapy to separate from his feelings. He can stand from a distance and watch them work through his nervous system, his psyche. He knows they are not facts but an emotional response to those truths. It can be fascinating to realize one's capability to split the mind in two and watch oneself think. It's fascinating but exhausting, and Frankie doesn't have the energy right now. He's just playing dumb and letting his emotions take the lead.

"The green chairs, really?"

Frankie turns to find Shane behind him, standing with his hands on his hips, head tipped to the side, a wrinkled smile on his lips. "They're ugly and uncomfortable."

Frankie feels the air rush back into his chest, as if he'd forgotten to breathe for a couple of months. He hates that seeing this man who hurt him so deeply still has the power to calm him.

"Like our relationship," Frankie says before he can stop himself.

"Wow," Shane says, eyes widening. "That didn't take long."

Frankie locks his hands together behind his back to avoid reaching for the past. He wants to ask a million questions, mainly about the boys, but that only invites more hurt. He misses how life felt when he believed all the lies, making him homesick for a mirage. Looking at Shane now, he's trying to see him as a stranger. He has glimpses of feeling absolutely nothing for the blandly handsome bag of assholes before him, but it's served with a chaser of missing the life they had together. Most of the time, if you didn't take the time to look too closely, it was a decent life.

Shane is watching him, waiting. It's got to be killing him to remain silent when he's famous for needing noise. There's always talking or music or television or humming when Shane is around. He claims he has tinnitus, so the sounds drown out the constant ringing in his ear. Frankie wonders now if that ringing isn't actually the inner voice of reason, suggesting he not be a selfish whore, and he doesn't want to hear what he doesn't want to know.

It's also possible he actually has tinnitus and doesn't give two shits about the carcass of Frankie's love he left in a ditch.

"Can you just walk with me for a bit and let me pretend the cheating and pain never happened?" Frankie asks, and Shane doesn't seem so sure.

"Oh, come on," Frankie adds. "At this point, what's one more lie?"

Shane dips his head, pained, but the look he gives Frankie isn't one of true remorse—it's more like a wounded child seeking pity. The sight of it ignites something hot in Frankie's chest, anger sparking where the hurt had been. Shane doesn't seem sorry; instead, he looks as though he expects Frankie to apologize for daring to be hurt. The realization that this might be closer to the truth than Shane would ever admit sharpens the edge of Frankie's frustration. He turns away abruptly, biting down on the urge to let a "sorry" escape his lips.

With every step, Frankie grinds his teeth, forcing himself not to glance back, not to hope for Shane to follow. But when Shane slips into his peripheral vision, elbow brushing against his, settling into step beside him, Frankie feels a surge of mixed emotions—relief tinged with bitterness. The relief stings, and that only makes him angrier.

"Have you heard from your mom?"

How dare Shane ask this? That is not his to care about. Their conversation must stay at the shallow end of the pool right now, or Frankie will quickly drown in emotional vulnerability. Worse, he will mistake Shane for a life preserver when he's really a cement boot. Frankie ignores the question and spits back with a forced casualness, "How's the new job?"

Shane takes the hint. "It's fine. I'm not traveling as much anymore, which is good for…"

Shane graciously lets "the boys" go unspoken. Frankie can't bear to hear about them. Not yet. Maybe not ever. They both know it.

Instead, Shane rambles on about work complications and financial struggles, his voice a familiar melody that Frankie craves and despises. "It's more complicated than expected," Shane says, hands buried deep in his pockets. "It's not as easy now that I'm down to a single-income household."

Frankie's chest tightens at the words. The urge to ask about the foreclosure burns on his tongue, but he swallows it. For once, he has a secret from Shane, and the power tastes bittersweet. It might hurt Shane to bring it up, which has appeal, but it could also lead to another series of lies that Frankie will want to believe. Best to leave it in the dark.

"I've started running," Shane continues. "Planning to do a 5K in the fall."

Another nerve is plucked. Frankie was always the runner, pounding pavements while Shane stayed home, likely working up a sweat with a stranger. Each syllable is a reminder of betrayal wrapped in the warmth of nostalgia.

Sensing correctly that even the simple things are hitting Frankie like razorblade kisses, Shane settles into his version of silence, which is to hum. Frankie immediately recognizes the melody as Slow Down by Rachael Sage, the indie singer-songwriter they discovered together, and it works the kind of dark magic Shane is famous for. It makes Frankie forget all the bad and only remember how it felt to drive with Shane somewhere, listening to the radio, their fingers interlocked over the gear shift. They would daydream out loud together about opening a restaurant or a bar, books they should turn into movies, remodeling the house, trips to wine country, the Maldives, the moon.

The memories make Frankie happy, which makes him

sad. Against his better judgment, he admits as much. "I hate you. And I miss you. Which makes me hate you more."

"Oh Frankie…"

Maybe Shane meant to take his hand or punch him in the chest. Instead, the kissing happens. There's anger and hurt and hunger in it, but with every taste of Shane's lips, Frankie feels cobwebs being blown out of the attic in his mind. Yes, his willpower might be burning down around him, but, by God, there is finally sunlight in the attic again! Maybe you must burn it all down so you can build again. Now, Frankie hates himself for thinking that maybe they can find their way back to each other. He pulls Shane closer, nearly knocking them both to the ground. Cars pass by, casting spotlights on the possibilities. Maybe they can fix this, can't they? Isn't love just about hanging in there, no matter what happens? Maybe. Maybe. Maybe.

Shane suddenly pulls back and gasps. "I can't do this." He turns away from Frankie, covering his face with his hands as if hiding from the moment.

"I know," Frankie says to Shane's back, fighting the urge to wrap his arms around him from behind. That's how they used to sleep, Frankie holding Shane, Shane facing away. The irony of the obvious hits him: Now, when Frankie most needs to turn away, he finds himself desperately wanting to hold on.

"I'm not gay," Shane finally says without looking at Frankie.

It takes history's longest minute for Frankie to realize Shane believes he's being honest, and it strikes Frankie as darkly humorous.

"Does your ass know that?" Frankie asks.

Shane is spinning in place, hands in and out of pockets as he struggles to explain. "After we broke up, I had the boys for a long weekend. They asked a lot about you and what happened. It was confusing for them. Remember when Brady asked if you were the lady? Anyway, when I took them home, Sherry knew something was wrong, and we started talking. I really opened up to her."

Frankie isn't sure where this is going, but it's bouncing off his insides like acid popcorn. "Like you opened up to half of Des Moines?"

"Stop it!" Shane snaps. "I'm trying to be honest with you."

"No wonder I don't recognize it."

Shane looks like he's been slapped, so Frankie dials it back, calming himself, though it's not lost on him that Shane deserves a slap. A real one. "Go on."

Shane tiptoes forward with his truth, his voice taking on a practiced, introspective tone. "I was on a journey of self-discovery, you know? Grappling with my authentic self. I realize now I was projecting my insecurities and acting out from a place of unresolved trauma."

Frankie is trying to just listen, but Shane's self-indulgent therapy-speak annoys the hell out of him. "And at what point did you find clarity?" he asks. "Because you didn't have it with Sherry, and you sure as hell didn't find it with me."

Shane sounds like he is delivering this speech like a shitty child actor in community theater. "I've done a lot of work in the last few months. Self-work. And I realized that the reason I kept searching beyond my marriage and then our relationship was, well, I was trying to fill a void."

Frankie swallows a zinger of a response: "Which you filled repeatedly." Instead, he watches Shane, noticing how he suddenly seems smaller with every tortured explanation.

Shane mistakes Frankie's expression for confusion, adding with self-righteousness, "I can't make you understand, but you still deserve to hear the truth."

Frankie can actually taste the blood from biting his lip.

"Sherry convinced me to seek out some therapy," Shane continues. Frankie finally gets a sense of where this is going. It would be hilarious if it wasn't shredding his insides.

"We've been working together on this, and, well, I've known Sherry for 17 years, and she's the mother of my children." He pauses as if he's asking Frankie if he actually wants to hear the next part. He doesn't, but he has to.

"Go ahead. Say it."

Shane raises his eyebrows as if to ask, "Are you sure?" and Frankie nods. Shane stammers, clearly not thinking through exactly how this part would feel. He clears his throat. "Well, even after everything I've put her through, she wants us to be a family. With therapy, I can right my wrong. I can make it work."

Frankie's mouth fills with battery acid, and the burning surge threatens to crumble his teeth into dust.

Shane looks as if he pities Frankie for not understanding. It's clear that he has arrived at the end of his rehearsed script and wants to deliver the climactic line just right.

"I want you to know…" he starts, but Frankie doesn't want to hear it. And the only way he can stop the droning of his newly enlightened ex is to deliver a punch to the middle of Shane's smug face.

26

STRINGS.

JULES CAN'T TELL IF Heidi is drunk or high or horny, but whatever she is, Jules is starting to question their friendship. Heidi is leaning against the counter, mostly watching Joshua talk to various people between acts. Jules watches how Heidi grits her teeth when Joshua smiles at any female passerby, and she suddenly understands Hollywood stalkers. "Keep walking, Darla," Heidi threatens under her breath as another woman nods toward Joshua. Jules notices that her friend is actually white-knuckling her wine spritzer. Jules wonders how quickly she could yank the bottle from Heidi's hand before she uses it as a weapon.

Tomias clears his throat in the microphone. "Okay, everyone. We're getting ready to wrap up. But I gotta try one more time: Maybe we have one last performance tonight? How about it, Joshua?"

The crowd erupts, and Joshua throws up his hands in

surrender, milking the moment as the applause swells. Jules notices how well he's learned to play the game. She watches him step up on stage as the audience goes wild, but Heidi's maniacal scream easily cuts through the applause. Jules feels herself openly glaring at her. "Please shut up," she says, wrapping her fingers around Heidi's wrist and digging her nails in enough to make Heidi whimper.

"Hey everybody," Joshua says with the Southern accent that he picked up somewhere in Nashville. "I hope you don't mind if I try out something new tonight."

The audience clearly doesn't mind. Jules feels the tickle of apprehension, wondering how long she can maintain this façade of cool. How long before Joshua blows a lethal kiss against the house of cards she's trying to keep in place?

"It's called *We Could Run*."

Shit. Jules feels tears creep to the corner of her eyes, even before he starts to sing. She resents the way he doesn't look in her direction as he plucks a couple of strings on the guitar, tuning it. The melody starts and falls squarely into a melancholy memory.

You are standing over there
I am trying not to stare
We are looking past each other
Trying to take cover
From the winds that want to tear us
from the things that we have done
We really shouldn't be here
Though the danger's kind of fun
Oh maybe baby
Maybe baby

Maybe baby

we

could

run.

Jules knows she can't pay too close attention or she'll give herself away, but it's too late. Tears slip down her cheeks, and she has to turn away from the stage. She can't let herself hear him.

She glances at the pass-through toward the back kitchen. Her dad and Mona are whispering to each other as they watch Joshua sing. Her dad catches her eye and gives a wink, nodding toward Joshua and giving her a thumbs up. He's probably saying, "This kid's got some talent," but maybe, just maybe, he's saying, "Do it. Run away with him." Which one would she rather hear?

Now that she's decided she can't look at Joshua or her father, Jules directs her attention out the front windows just in time to see Frankie approach the front door propped open by the crowd. His energy resembles a bag of dynamite thrown on a campfire. He looks broken in a new way. It immediately pisses her off. Jesus, now what? She's exhausted from picking up the pieces around her brother while her own shattering keeps going unnoticed by every goddamn person around her.

Frankie looks like he can't decide which direction to go. He turns to head in the direction he had come but then changes his mind and moves toward the front door. A second later, Shane steps into the frame of the window. Jules is confused because it looks like Shane has a bloody nose. Not that he doesn't deserve one, but what the hell?

Frankie leans against the frame of the open front door

as Joshua finishes his song. Jules wonders if her brother even realizes his surroundings. Hugo stands two feet to his left. He came in earlier, asking Jules if Frankie was around. They'd been together earlier, and something had happened that Hugo needed to explain. Frankie had slipped out the back, apparently to talk to Shane, who now stands a few feet behind Frankie, wiping the blood from his upper lip.

Everything about Frankie's demeanor suggests he is about to collapse, but only Jules recognizes the warning signs. As the audience applauds Joshua's big finish, she starts toward Frankie. Just then, Joshua, oblivious to Frankie's cave-in, calls him up on stage.

"Frankie Parker! Come up here, man! I'm sure we have time for one more if you'll join me."

The crowd cheers again, and Jules wants to love how they are applauding for her brother, not just Joshua. These people love Frankie. Or at least they love who he was before the damage took hold. But Frankie's in trouble right now. He shakes off the heartfelt attention, but the audience is relentless, and it makes Jules sad for her brother. Sometimes kindness can be cruel.

Frankie starts to turn frantically toward the door to leave, but when he sees Shane, it sends him in the other direction. The crowd mistakes this for surrendering to their desires and nearly carries him to the stage. Jules, her hand clamped in panic over her mouth, can only watch what will happen next. Maybe, just maybe, their clapping will, Peter Pan style, transform him back to his previous self.

Placing Frankie on the stage, the audience is suddenly confused as he stands awkwardly, silently next to Joshua.

Sensing his friend's uneasiness, Joshua wraps his arm around Frankie and whispers something in his ear. Frankie gives a half-smile, nodding. Joshua slips the guitar strap over his head and slides it over Frankie. Frankie steps up to the microphone and clears his throat as he toys with the strings absentmindedly. Looking down, he laughs a little.

"Shit," he blurts into the microphone. "This won't work. I'm left-handed."

Some uneasy chuckles bounce around the audience as everyone waits.

Frankie exhales loudly into the microphone as his eyes scan the room. Landing on Jules, he gives her a wrinkled smile that she reads as a kind of apology. She kisses her hand and gives him a small wave. Frankie's voice begins to flow, tentative but growing in strength.

The crowd starts to cheer but falls silent as he works through a jarring a capella cover of Alanis Morissette's *You Outta Know*. It's rage-filled like the original but more bluesy and broken. It feels less "fuck you" and more "fuck this."

When he finishes, the applause is uncertain until Heidi lets out a whoop and shouts, "Hell, yeah!" The audience then cheers and claps. Frankie smiles weakly and glances toward the front door. Jules follows his eye to the space where Shane had been standing. Frankie doesn't realize it, but Hugo has also left.

It's clear it wasn't the rousing finale the crowd had been hoping for in the presence of a homegrown country star, but they take their proper cue and wrap up their stay. An hour later, the café is nearly empty, and clean-up is underway. Jules trades her red dress for sweatpants and one of Damon's old

T-shirts. She feels guilty wearing it, smelling him close to her, but it's the kind of shame she deserves.

She attempts to approach Frankie several times, but the way he pauses what he's doing to glance at her feet, not even her face, lets her know to stay away for now. He's wired and cleaning up quickly. Reorganizing the chairs, and wiping down the tables and bar, he finishes with the trash collected by the back door, all in the time it takes Jules to get the cooler restocked with ice. She calls to check on Sophie. As Damon recounts their evening of Disney princesses and grilled cheese, he sounds much farther than three miles away. When he asks about open mic night, she focuses on Thea's shitty song about duck sex because the rest of it is more than Jules is willing to admit.

As she hangs up, she notices Frankie sliding into a chair in the middle of the café, his energy skidding to a stop. He stares ahead, clearly unfocused.

Her attention is pulled away when she hears a cursed grumble from Clayton, followed by Mona laughing. Her dad emerges from the kitchen area with Mona behind him, patting him on the back. The front of his shirt is drenched with water. "You could have mentioned the sink sprayer was broken," he tells his daughter.

"Oh yeah," she replies flatly, biting her cheek. "Dad, the sink sprayer is broken."

He huffs a cartoonish "Well, I oughta" before pulling her into a damp hug. "You're doing good here, Kid."

The comment makes her hate herself a little because it's focused on who he thinks she is and not who she knows herself to be. Jules starts to push away from him but reconsiders; she relaxes into her father's arms. He instinctively rocks her a little while he rests his chin on the top of her head.

Clayton looks over toward Frankie and nods generously. "You too, son. It's a nice place."

Jules is lost in the safety net of her father's arms and misses whatever Frankie says. But suddenly, Clayton is enraged. His body turns to barbed wire so quickly that Jules pulls back, feeling the heat of his rage.

"What did you say?" Her father bellows in a way Jules hasn't heard since the time Frankie came home drunk and belligerent at 16.

Jules looks at Frankie, pleading with her eyes for him to take back whatever he just said to their father. Frankie looks pointedly at Clayton and enunciates disdainfully, "I said, 'Mom isn't coming home.' "

Clayton moves toward him like a lightning bolt. Frankie gets up, sending his chair flying toward the back wall. He stands his ground and says, "Everyone else knows it. You're the only one stupid enough to still wait for her. She turned you into an idiot. I hate that I learned from you that I should only love the unlovable."

The tension in the room feels like an execution trial. The pain on Clayton's face ricochets off Frankie's icy eyes, cracking the surface enough to give a glimpse of the ache hidden inside. When he was 16, the whipping he received would probably get Clayton arrested today. This time, Clayton doesn't need his hands to leave a mark. "If you ever speak of your mother like that again, I will kill you."

He turns to Mona with an "I'm leaving" and walks out. Mona discards the few bits of paper trash she had gathered and follows him, giving Jules an apologetic wave as she goes.

Frankie stands stone-still in the middle of the room.

"Why did you have to say that?" Jules asks him.

Frankie is still staring after their father long after he's gone. When he turns to Jules, his expression is as flat as his words. "I'll mop if you'll take out the trash."

The only proper response is to shrug in agreement. A few minutes later, she barges out the back door and props it open with the broken brick saved for such purposes. She hoists the first bag up into the dumpster and it leaks garbage juice down her arm. She realizes what an asshole Frankie was for offering to mop while she dragged the bags to the alley. She hates mopping, and he knows it. It seemed like a generous offer. She was wrong. He sucks.

Annoyed that Frankie manipulated her again, she wipes off her arm with the bar towel tucked in the waistband of her sweats. She reaches back into the café to open the bottom drawer of the desk. She flips up the lid on a small metal box with her thumb and reaches inside for the pack of cigarettes hidden there.

After slipping back outside, the sin stick has barely passed her lips when she's interrupted. "My, how the judgy have fallen."

Joshua knows full well he's a much more dangerous vice than any cigarette could ever be, but she tries to act casual. "Shut up. I'm not going to light it. Sometimes, I just like to feel it in my mouth."

He leans against the brick wall with way too much James Dean cool. "Am I really supposed to have no response to that?"

She shrugs him off because she has to and tosses another

garbage bag into the dumpster. Joshua helps with the next bag, and she has to pretend she isn't grateful or she's done for. The bag is heavier than he realizes, throwing his balance off. Joshua crashes into Jules, knocking her against the brick wall. He's fast enough to catch himself before slamming his full weight against her. She is trapped between his arms, and he stammers an apology but doesn't pull back.

"Sorry," he says.

She is too stunned to repeat the word, mostly because she isn't. She's too busy imagining what it would feel like to wrap her legs around him. To pull him close. To hide in what they could be together.

Both are winded, but Joshua is the one who breathes heavily. She wants to smile but uses her last bit of self-control to hold back. His breath is thick with mint, hiding his own smoking habit. It angers her and turns her on in equal measure. He looks at her for a long time. Jules wants to read his face like Braille, but instead, she digs her fingers into the bricks behind her, feeling the skin on her knuckles peel away. He leans forward as if to kiss her, and she leans forward as if to accept, but they both stop at the edge of a line neither is ready to cross, though it would take the jaws of life to separate them at this point.

Joshua suddenly looks as terrified as she feels. "Are we in trouble?"

She doesn't need to kiss him. She only needs to nod.

27

CUE.

CLAYTON WEAVES THROUGH town, following Mona back to her house. Mona said she didn't need an escort, but he insisted, maybe more for his well-being than any risk of her not getting home safely. He wasn't ready to be alone with his thoughts.

But on the drive, those thoughts weren't in the mood to be ignored. He knows Frankie isn't alone in what he thinks, but no one knows Carol like he does. She has always been full of surprises, and he knows, needs to know, that she'll be back tomorrow with stories and laughter to fill his heart.

It took a long time for Clayton to recognize love. His parents had been cordial and kind to each other, but nothing about their behavior resembled what young Clayton would see at the movies. His parents would sit on either side of him, not together where they might accidentally touch. He would hear his father silently grouse if the story had the nerve to veer toward romance. God forbid it be a musical. "If I ever saw someone burst into song and dance while walking down the street, they would meet the good end of my foot right away. It's just so absurd."

Clayton's father didn't believe in absurdity. He believed in cattle and corn. His mistress was the weather, and his family was expected to behave as an extension of him. Thoughts brought to the table that he didn't agree with were disregarded outright. And things he didn't understand were dismissed as absurd rather than admitting any confusion. Clayton cringes to imagine his father living in the electronic age. A gadget the size of a fist that fits in a pocket and costs less than a bicycle yet is more powerful than the first space shuttle? Not only is it nonsense, but it's also offensive. Speaking of offensive, he shudders at his father's likely reaction to learning Frankie was gay.

When Clayton's father died suddenly of a stroke at age 59 while pushing baby Frankie on a swing, Clayton watched his mother wrap up in the cocoon of grief and then emerge a widow butterfly. She shaved off the hair dye and embraced a cropped gray style that took nothing to manage. Her overalls and boots were replaced by bright caftans and sandals. She learned to throw pottery, speak Italian, and belly dance, and she died in her sleep while on a cruise in Belize at age 91. Clayton's father had spent maybe 12 hours of his life beyond the state borders, let alone exploring a different country.

After struggling to understand the changes in her following his father's death, Clayton finally asked her why she was so different. She only replied, "That's what love does to you."

He tried to push her for more, but she refused to elaborate and turned her attention to whatever new craft had taken her fancy.

Carol Rasmussen was a different breed. She came from romance, and she looked like the cover of a romance novel. Elizabeth Taylor beautiful, with the same fiery spirit. Her parents were amorous in ways built to humiliate their children and make the furniture blush. Carol had chosen Clayton, perhaps as a project. She repeatedly took him by surprise and pushed him to talk about his feelings, to acknowledge they were real. She told him that she loved him on their first date. It wasn't even a formal date. They had crossed paths at the county fair, and she asked him to join her on the Ferris wheel. She was beautiful, and Clayton didn't understand why she had picked him, but he said yes. High in the sky, she rocked their chair to the point that Clayton was certain they were going to die. When he told her as much, she cackled with laughter and kicked her legs out into the sky.

"I've decided to love you, Clayton Parker," she announced to the sky and the cotton candy she waved like a pom-pom. "But you need a little work, my boy. I do hope you're up for the task because this kind of love can't wait forever."

It took him almost a year to say it back to her, and even then, the words felt funny in his mouth, like maybe he was pronouncing it wrong. She pursed her lips when he said it, suggesting she wasn't yet convinced. She made him say it again over the next few months until she finally believed him.

Now, he follows as Mona pulls into the driveway and parks. She waves to him as the automatic garage door slides down. He moves the truck into reverse to leave when he realizes she is waving him in. Clayton glances to the passenger seat, feeling the eyes of judgment from Carol once again. He shakes the image from his head, feels a spark of rebellion, and parks, jumping out to follow Mona toward the house.

"Would you like a nightcap? A coffee? Mylanta?"

He chuckles with a boyish shrug. "I'm not sure."

"Ah," she says. "My favorite."

She struggles to find the right key, holding a custodian's jangle up to the streetlight until she finds the one with the red tag and slips it into no fewer than three locks. "I know it's stupid. One key for three locks. If you've got this key, you can get in so why bother? I don't know. Faith in the ignorance of others, I guess."

She leads him in, and Clayton is struck with the memory of walking through this same door in a black suit, so it must have been for Joey's funeral. Clayton expects they are headed for the kitchen. Instead, Mona clicks on a light and leads him down to the basement. The ceilings are higher than expected, and Clayton is surprised to realize there is a walkout basement. Two sliding glass doors at the end of the family room lead out into the dark. From the front of the house, there is no indication there's a slope to the backyard.

Mona clicks on more lights, revealing a mahogany bar and a stained-glass lamp over a pool table. She slips behind the bar to pour two glasses of expensive-looking whiskey.

"I never drank this stuff while married, but he fought me for it in the divorce. So now I love it," she says.

Mona hands Clayton a glass and toasts him. "Well, tonight was fun, right?"

He chuckles ruefully and takes a sip. It's rich and strong,

smoky and sharp. A welcoming burn moves down his throat and reaches his toes.

He sets the glass on the edge of the pool table and grabs the cue ball. Soft classical music slinks in like a mellow whisper. Mona comes out from behind the bar, and he suddenly feels like there should be more space between them, so he moves around to the opposite side of the pool table. Absent-mindedly, he starts rolling the ball across the table, bouncing it off the other side so it comes back to his open hand.

Mona reaches for the 8-ball and mirrors him, rolling her ball back and forth. "Wanna talk about what happened?"

"No, I don't."

Her face sags, and he regrets his brusqueness.

As a peace offering, he adds, "I feel like I don't know anything anymore."

"Yeah," Mona says, full of understanding. "Seems about right."

It's quiet for a long time. Clayton prefers the silence, but Mona has more to say.

"After Joey died, Roger and I just drifted apart. He's not a bad man, but that doesn't mean he was a good father or husband."

"I don't see how there's a difference."

Mona sucks an ice cube and nods in agreement. "Probably not, but it's easier to admit I loved that bastard if I convince myself there is."

Clayton feels his eyes start to itch like he has a tickle in his brain. He suddenly remembers being here another time before. It was many years ago. Mona and Roger were dressed up, she with a pale-yellow corsage and him with a matching boutonniere. Carol was wearing a new dress—an argument that Clayton had lost. In protest, he was in an old suit. Carol's corsage was a pale purple. The occasion was Jules's eighth-grade dance. They had all been chaperones and met for a drink before heading to the school.

Why was Clayton remembering that night now? The way Carol swayed to every song and begged Clayton to dance? On his third refusal, she took Roger by the hand and led him to the dance floor. Clayton hadn't felt jealous in his marriage before that night, but something about how Carol's hand rested on Roger's shoulder offended him. To spite her, he had invited Mona to dance and held her closer than the nuns would have allowed when he was a boy. "Keep room for the Holy Spirit," they would say, yanking the boys and girls to a respectable distance. There was nothing respectable about how he held Mona that night, the way he remembers her fingertips pressed into his shoulder as they danced, and about how he recalled thinking about her later that night. And many times after that. Until he told himself to forget about her, which he had somehow managed to do.

"I should go," he suddenly says when he realizes his glass is empty of even the memory of ice.

"Okay," she says.

But neither of them moves other than to roll their pool balls. They roll again, and the room echoes with a crack as white meets black in the middle of the table. They are both still for a moment.

There is much involved in leaving: stairs to climb, the back door, the walk to the truck, and the 40-minute drive home. It is more than Clayton is ready for.

"Can we sit for a minute?" he asks.

"Of course we can," Mona replies as she flips a switch that brings a gas fireplace to life. She retrieves two blankets from a footstool trunk and hands one to him. He looks at the quilt in Mona's outstretched hand. It feels wrong to be here, but right now, he wouldn't want to be anywhere else.

He takes it from her and follows her to two chairs flanking the fireplace. "I don't know why I turned it on," she says, nodding toward the fire. "It's the middle of summer."

"I like the light," Clayton says as he settles into a chair while she sinks into the one across from him.

She studies him for a moment and then says, "I would like to say something that you might not want to hear."

He doesn't say anything, hoping she won't continue. He wants to stay in the silence, but he knows he can't. He waits a moment longer, holding onto the quiet, fearing that whatever she says will make him like her less, and he's not ready for that. Finally, he glances up at her and nods.

She pauses, choosing her words carefully. "I wish for you to be waiting for someone who chooses you."

"Carol's coming home," he reiterates for the hundredth time.

"I'm not suggesting she isn't," Mona says. "I simply want you to feel like a priority and not an option."

Clayton looks away, his jaw tightening as he absorbs her words. "Carol's always had her own way of doing things," he says, his voice a little rough. "It doesn't mean I'm not, we're not important to her. She just… she needs her space sometimes."

He pauses, the weight of Mona's statement lingering in the air. "I know she loves me," he adds quietly, turning to watch the flames flicker in the fireplace before looking back to Mona. "Isn't that enough?"

Mona's eyes soften. "Maybe it is." She pulls the blanket higher up her legs and changes the subject. "Can we talk about that fucking duck song for a second?"

Clayton laughs so loud and abruptly that it actually hurts his ribcage, and he must lean forward to catch his breath. When his breathing feels stable again, he leans back, wiping laughter's tears from his eyes.

"Yes," he says with a sigh of great release. "Yes, we can."

28

WANT.

THERE'S SOMETHING SEDUCTIVE about being destructive. Frankie knows this, but he'd forgotten about the variety of destructive behaviors that exist. Not all of them had to feel shitty. Some of them could feel like dancing. In fact, dance itself could feel destructive. At least, that's what it felt like from the middle of the dance floor at Curfew.

This club in the warehouse district has been around for longer than Frankie has been alive, at least longer than he had realized he was gay, which is basically the same thing. Frankie is wildly out of shape after months of moving files from one place to another and carrying around the weight of the world on his shoulders being his only exercise. But he is dancing. He can barely breathe, and everything hurts, but he is dancing.

The dance floor is crowded, and the DJ has the bass so thick that it makes the earth shake. Frankie leans into the bodies around him and closes his eyes. It feels good to be touched, even if there is nothing intimate or intentional about it. But suddenly, a hand claps his shoulder. He opens his eyes to find Bobby leaning close to shout over the music. "Well, well, well, twice in one day. Aren't I lucky?"

Frankie lets his eyes fall over Bobby's naughty Boy Scout face, the tease of chest hair over his tight T-shirt that is nearly transparent from sweat. His pants have a porn star fit that's borderline offensive. Luckily, Frankie is in the mood to be offended.

They dance together for a bit, close and physical. Frankie lets the music carry him out of his comfort zone, and he slides his hands up Bobby's shirt, feeling his muscles and chest. He loops his fingers up over the neck opening on Bobby's shirt, and pulls him closer. Bobby's hands are exploring Frankie's back pockets.

Bobby leans in and nibbles Frankie on the neck, whispering something that Frankie can't hear, but he laughs hard and loud anyway, running his fingers through Bobby's sweaty hair, pulling a little more aggressively than needed. He doesn't care. And the giddy look on Bobby's face suggests he welcomes the rough treatment. It's crazy to think that 24 hours ago, Bobby was little more than a beige blur as Frankie's boss, and now they are breaking all kinds of HR rules.

Out of the corner of his eye, Frankie senses someone watching him. He glances over; the strobe lights make it difficult to tell, but he's sure someone is looking at him. It seems to be coming from a small group of men around a table at the edge of the dance floor. Frankie tries to ignore it, but the feeling pulls at the back of his head as aggressively as

Bobby pulls at the top of his jeans. He looks again, and this time it's clear. Hugo stands with a group of pretty boys, but he's obviously watching Frankie. There's something painful about his expression, and Frankie feels pangs of guilt. But why should he? Hugo was a stranger until today—a stranger who turned out to be a liar.

Frankie wants to be annoyed and angry and tries to force those emotions, pushing harder into Bobby, but it's pointless. He's not annoyed and angry. He's sad and tired.

He pulls away from Bobby, and they return to dancing separately. He glances at Hugo and sees that he's now talking to Andrew, but they both look in his direction. Fed up, Frankie waits for Bobby to turn away from him and then uses the opportunity to dip off the dance floor in the opposite direction from Hugo.

He snakes his way through the side hallway, forcing quick hellos and hugs to people he pretends to remember. He pushes by the line of people waiting to get in to make his escape.

There's a nip in the air as he crosses the street to his car, his sweat attracting the chill. He stabs the key into the door when he hears his name and stops.

Hugo runs across the street to him. "Frankie, please listen—"

Frankie tries to push Hugo hard in the chest, but Hugo's forward momentum from running knocks Frankie back against the car next to his, setting off the blaring alarm.

"No, you listen!" Frankie screams over the screaming. "Do you have any idea how hard it was to let my guard down? You saw what a mess I was this morning, and you used it against me!"

Hugo reaches out for Frankie but reads the risk in Frankie's body language and steps back instead. "You don't understand—"

"I don't want to understand!" Frankie feels the tears shredding his voice, making him even angrier with himself, with Hugo, and with the world. "I'm tired of trying to understand. I can't wrap my head around why you turned me into a joke today."

Hugo's eyes fill with desperation, but he stops, settles back, and shakes his head. "You can't hear me at all, can you?"

"Oh, but I do," Frankie says, unable to take his eyes off that beautiful mouth. But just to drive the stake in, he adds, "Loud and clear, you fucking faggot."

The alarm suddenly goes quiet, as if the car was stunned by Frankie's cruelty. Hugo's eyes are teary. He sighs and shakes his head before finally saying, "Goodbye, Frankie."

An apology claws at the back of Frankie's throat, but he swallows it and gets in his car. As he drives away, he tries to stare at the road ahead but can't ignore the sight of Hugo in the rearview mirror, standing in the middle of the street, watching him leave.

Frankie should just go home; that couldn't be more obvious. But he's not ready to be wise, not yet. The chaos in his mind won't let him settle. Thoughts collide like they're trying to tear through him. His heart pounds so hard he can feel it in his throat, and his vision blurs around the edges. He pulls to the side of the road, the streetlights casting harsh shadows through the windshield. He leans his head back against the seat and screams against all the confusion, hurt, fear, doubt, love. He wants it out of him, all of it.

He closes his eyes and wills himself to breathe, but the breaths come out ragged, unsteady.

He fumbles for his phone and checks it without really knowing why. There are no messages or missed calls. He doesn't want to hear from anyone, and yet the silence stings. With a frustrated grunt, he tosses the phone onto the passenger seat and looks out the window.

He's in the East Village, where life carries on around him. The streets are alive with Saturday night revelers, their laughter floating on the cool night air, mingling with the clinking of glasses and the hum of conversation. Couples and groups of friends lean into each other, sharing jokes and secrets, their joy a sharp contrast to the storm raging inside him. It all feels surreal as if he's watching a movie he's not a part of. The world outside his car is vibrant and full of life, while inside, he's crumbling, barely holding it together.

He watches a couple stumble out of a bar, arms wrapped around each other, faces flushed with alcohol and happiness. The sight of their easy affection twists something in his gut.

His hands tighten on the steering wheel until his knuckles turn white. He wants to scream again, to pound his fists against the dashboard, to do anything to release the pressure building inside him. But he knows it won't help; it never does. The anger, the sadness, the frustration—they're all part of the same tangled mess that's been inside him for too long. He doesn't know how to deal with it, how to untangle the knots inside his chest without unraveling completely. So, he sits there, breathing hard, eyes squeezed shut, trying to hold himself together for just a little longer. He feels like he's on the edge of something big, something that might break him if he's not careful.

The noise of the city feels distant now, muted by the pounding in his head. He puts the car in drive and starts to pull away, determined to do the right thing and take himself home, away from the temptations to feel the crash and burn. As he turns his head to check the traffic, he realizes that he's sitting across from Nowhere Bar, and it makes him pause. This is the bar where he first stepped out of the closet, where his life as an out gay man began. Maybe it holds the key to starting over from the mess he's in now. It's a dangerous ask from the universe, but that doesn't stop him from putting the van in park and unbuckling his seatbelt. As he opens the door, the air outside flickers with energy that should push him back into his seat but instead pulls him like a magnet across the street.

The closer he gets to the entrance, the louder the music becomes, and a low thrum vibrates through the pavement, pulsing under his feet. He pauses for a second, just outside the door. Frankie knows this is a mistake and knows he's walking a dangerous line, but at this moment, he doesn't care. He just needs to forget, if only for a little while longer.

29

SETTING.

Jules read once that the reason hotel bedspreads often have loud and busy prints is because it's easier to hide the stains. Mistakes get lost in the distraction. That makes sense now as she sits on the bed in Joshua's swanky hotel room. Her host leans on the windowsill with city lights twinkling behind him. They haven't spoken in nearly an hour, but they also haven't left each other's side since he helped her close the café. Without discussion, she had followed him to his truck, to his hotel, to his room.

He had slid off his boots as they entered the room. Jules didn't follow suit in case she suddenly had the wherewithal to run. Joshua seemed to catch the indication and chuckled a little but didn't say anything. She plopped down on the edge of the bed and let her legs fall open more than her mother would deem appropriate. She didn't mind the idea of offending her mother since she blames her mother for passing along the itchiness that prompted Jules to find herself here.

Joshua's arms cross his chest so that he's holding his opposite shoulders. It makes Jules smile because this is what he'd look like in a straitjacket. Certifiably insane and still hot as hell.

Jules took Joshua's virginity in high school, but he didn't take hers, a point of contention back in the day. Everyone assumed Joshua had had sex with Bambi Walcott because they dated for two years, were sickening with the PDA, and she had the tits, tricks, and lips to carry a name like Bambi Walcott. Yet no one realized that Jules was getting all kinds of education from her chemistry lab partner, Hank Slacks, because they never formally dated, didn't knowingly speak to each other in school outside of class, and he had the wits, charm, and zits to deserve a name like Hank Slacks.

When Joshua and Jules started dating, he assumed she was a virgin, and she assumed he was not. She read his sexual apprehension as a lack of interest. Frankie teased her that it probably meant Joshua was gay. She ignored her brother's gaydar because it was a superpower he hadn't yet honed, instead pointing it at any male with the hope it would lessen the weight of his loneliness. Joshua finally asked her if she was sure she was ready, and she offered a snarky "duh" as a reply. Finally, she had the hottest guy in school on top of her … and then under her. He was pleasantly surprised to learn all the lessons she had taken from Hank Slacks, and she was thrilled with the prospect of discovering how all these things might feel with someone who made her heart and head feel as hungry as her body.

Given where her mind has gone, and her body now sits,

it's startling to hear herself suddenly say, "I'm not unhappy in my life."

The statement seems to wander around the room, resetting all the upturned questions and doubts that have been kicked around between them ever since he walked into Fuel Injector. Jules looks around as if watching the remark take shape as a fact rather than a hope.

"Are you sure?" Joshua asks, justifiably doubting her, given the circumstances.

She nods, surprised to find she is sure. Very sure.

"It's not the life I imagined," she tells him. "But it's the life that I have."

He uncrosses his arms as he considers this, wrinkling his nose in protest. "That sounds like settling."

Jules rolls her eyes a little. "What does that even mean?"

Jules has always been bothered by the concept of "settling." It sounds like judgment against someone who has the audacity to find peace in a life different from the one they daydreamed of as a kid. But she's glad Joshua brought it up because it's helping clarify questions she didn't even know she was asking.

"There's a fine line between settling and acceptance. Just because my life is different from what I expected doesn't mean it's wrong." She knows she's sounding more brittle, more brutal than she intended. "Besides, happiness is overrated. Real life is work; it's not recess."

He laughs. "Be careful. Whatever you say may be used against you in a country song."

She sighs as she feels the shift in the room. Something is leaving. A feeling, a fear, is evaporating. Jules needs something to change, but not like this. Joshua feels it, too, and comes to sit next to her on the bed. "This isn't going to happen, is it?" he asks sadly.

She turns to look at him. He's so beautiful that it makes her heart hurt. She brushes the hair off his forehead. "No, it's not."

He slumps down a bit, flashing a pout that used to be his calling card in high school. "Once upon a time, we could have been perfect."

"Nah," she says and hugs him. When Joshua hugs her back, it doesn't feel exciting; it feels like family. "We were always a big stack of maybes. At this point in life, I prefer being sure."

She feels him laugh against her. "Well, that's definitely going to be a country song."

They pull away from each other, and she studies his face to make sure she's sure. "You'll always be one of my favorite people."

She realizes that this is more complicated than she expected. She had anticipated how saying yes to this would mess up her life, but she forgot to consider how saying no to this would bring out this color of hurt in Joshua's eyes. He blinks it away, trying to pretend that Jules doesn't know him like he knows she does. He huffs his chest and stands to step away from her, accepting what has become clear.

"You gonna come see me at the fair?" he asks, friend to friend. "Bring your family backstage. Meet Miranda Lambert."

Suddenly, Jules is eager to get home. She's got a baby girl to kiss and a husband to dance with in the kitchen while he burns dinner. When the life you have reveals itself as the life you want, it can be hard to sit still in anything else.

"Maybe," she says, standing up and brushing off her skirt. "I gotta go."

He doesn't respond right away, testing her resolve. "I wish you didn't seem so sure of that."

She's already moving toward the door. This suddenly feels so stupid. What the hell is she doing here?

"Goodbye, my friend," he says, sadness tripping up his words a bit.

The statement warms her, and as she opens the door, she can't help but lean back and kiss him again on the cheek. It breaks her heart a little, and that's okay. No one promised that the right choice would be easy. He turns his lips toward hers, but she declines the invitation. He takes her hand, and they slowly step back from each other until their fingertips are just barely touching over the threshold of the doorway. His smile is sad but sweet, and she starts to give in, tipping forward on her toes, but she stops herself and lowers her hand, leaning back against the wall away from him, rediscovering her balance. She doesn't make a sound as she mouths, "Goodbye."

Joshua dares her for a moment longer and then winks before shutting the door.

Jules stares at the door for a moment, wondering what the future looks like in an alternative universe where she makes a different choice. As the sketches start to fill in with detail and color, she shakes them off. She doesn't care about some other future. She wants this one. She wants to go home.

She turns and nearly collapses when she finds Damon standing in the middle of the hall in his bedtime sweatpants and the T-shirt she slept in when he was out of town, a sleeping Sophie wrapped up in his arms. His eyes are bloodshot, and tears streak his face. Without saying anything, he steps forward and hands Jules a photo strip of Jules and Joshua as teenagers. Laughing, loving, stupid. She has no idea where he found it. Maybe in the box she spilled in the garage. Maybe when she was looking for the recipe for the pineapple pie. Maybe it doesn't matter.

She looks at him, lost for words, only able to whisper, "I can't believe you brought her."

His lip shakes. "I can't believe that's the most shocking thing about this moment."

Tears break free from both of them as they look at each other, wanting truths to turn to water and wash away the hurt.

"It's not what it looks like," she begs.

He stares at her for a moment, gently shifting Sophie so as not to wake her.

"The end never is."

He walks away, and Jules knows not to chase him. All she can do is watch her baby girl's sleeping face as they fade into the distance.

She looks back at Joshua's door, wondering if she should knock, slip back inside to hide, and follow through on the mistakes that can create such sensual distractions. Instead, she follows in Damon's direction. She walks slowly at first as if wanting to respect his dramatic exit, but then she picks up the pace until she's running.

She just misses the elevator, so she takes the stairs instead. Luckily, Joshua is only on the fourth floor; much more than that would have tested her lung capacity. She makes it to the lobby in time to see Damon carrying Sophie through the sliding doors leading outside.

Racing after them, she reaches Damon's car just as he carefully, quietly, gets Sophie locked into her car seat. As he gently clicks the door shut, he turns to the noise of Jules's shoes carrying her across the cement. "Nothing happened," she says, her voice clipped with emotion.

"That's not exactly true, is it?" he asks, and she can't deny some wrongdoing.

"No," she says. "I've been feeling lost for a while. I could blame my mother and the last few months, but that's just an excuse."

Damon leads her away from the car so they don't wake Sophie. He studies Jules before speaking. "We have felt broken for longer than your mother has been gone."

She starts to shake her head but can't deny what he's saying and stops.

He continues, "I don't know if I want to do this anymore."

The calmness in his words is more devastating than the words themselves, and she is stunned into silence as he moves back toward the car.

"Go to your father's tonight," he says. "Be there for him tomorrow."

"But what about us?" she asks.

"I don't know," he says without looking at her. He reaches for his door but turns back. "Good luck tomorrow."

The tears streaming down Jules's face drown her ability to respond, so she only nods. Damon gets in the car and pulls away, leaving Jules standing in the dark long after his rear lights have disappeared.

SUNDAY

30

UNCOVERED.

FRANKIE IS DROWNING in a sea of blankets, thrashing and grunting as he tries to claw his way to the surface. The weight of the covers is oppressive like they're trying to pull him back into unconsciousness. His head feels like it's been filled with angry bees, buzzing and stinging with every movement, and it's so heavy he can barely lift it from the pillow. He catches a glimpse of light on the far side of the bed—a sliver of hope in an otherwise dark and unfamiliar place. If he can just reach it, maybe he can make sense of where he is, but it's like dragging his body through wet cement.

It takes all his strength to crawl what feels like a thousand miles to the edge of the bed. When he finally peeks over, his eyes struggle to focus. Instead of the familiar comfort of his childhood bedroom, he's met with something that makes his stomach lurch—a mannequin head covered in shards of disco ball glass stares back at him, its hollow eyes casting a fractured reflection of his confusion.

The room is bathed in an eerie, fragmented light, beams of sunshine bouncing off the mirror shards and scattering across the walls, the ceiling, and the floor. It's a dizzying, disorienting effect, as if he's trapped inside a kaleidoscope. The rest of the room slowly comes into focus, and what he sees sends another wave of nausea through him. The décor is jarringly overdone, like a caricature of every gay stereotype he's ever seen—a meticulously curated shrine to style, precision, and artifice. A disco ball hangs from the ceiling, casting tiny rainbow-colored spots across the room. The bed he's in is draped in velvet, a deep shade of burgundy that seems to swallow the light. On the nightstand, a bouquet of peacock feathers sprays out of a crystal vase, standing next to a small army of perfectly aligned designer colognes. The walls are adorned with glossy, black-and-white photographs of scantily clad men, their poses deliberately provocative. If "Gay Cliché" were a magazine, this would be the centerfold.

The mannequin's mirrored eyes catch the sunlight again, and for a moment, he feels like he's being watched, judged, for his snarled lip by this lifeless figure. The surreal quality of the room closes in on him, making it hard to breathe. He has to get out—now.

He makes his way to his feet, which takes every bit of energy he has. Every sound he makes, every creak and crack of his body, is magnified inside his thumping head. Did he break something? Shouldn't he be in a body cast? Or be hooked up to a morphine drip?

He suddenly needs to pee. As he opens the door, he smells coffee in the air. Pee, then coffee, he decides. Somewhere in there, he'll figure out where the hell he is.

He staggers to a bathroom and lets out a startled yelp at the blood-shot, hungover beast that greets him in the mirror. No time to deal with that when one's got to empty the boot. He pees for so long that his knees threaten to buckle. Frankie controls his aim with one hand, while the other keeps him balanced against the frosted mirror shelving unit surrounding the toilet.

He washes his hands and shakes them dry, suspicious of the hand towels, which look plastic rather than plush. Then he goes back to the bedroom to gather his clothes, which are neatly folded in a zebra-print chair so low to the ground that Frankie has to brace his hand on his back to lower himself to reach them.

Pulled together as best as he's going to manage, Frankie heads in the direction of banging pots and pans. Down a short hallway, he is greeted by Bobby darting around a galley kitchen, dealing with what may or may not be a grease fire on the stove. Frankie picks up a metal lid and places it on top of the flaming pan, removing it to reveal no more fire. Bobby looks at him with question-mark eyes. "Science," Frankie replies and looks for coffee, only to find one of those single-cup pod machines he has never liked.

Sensing his displeasure, Bobby makes it for Frankie, setting a mug, picking a pod, pop drop plop, steam heat. "Good morning," he says with a little bounce in his hip toward Frankie.

"Morning," Frankie replies, not quite sure which adjective is appropriate. He glances around the kitchen, curious about the life of this person that he has worked with for months and had sex with a few hours ago, though, technically, the term "sex" may not officially apply, depending on who you ask. The details tumble forth as he watches the coffee brew. Orgasms? Yes. Penetration? No. Regret? Definitely.

Frankie studies Bobby as he moves around the kitchen, trying to define why he feels so milquetoast in this morning light. It could be the fog of shame, exhaustion, and 10 drinks too many, but there's something else going on that Frankie's trying to piece together. It's not that Bobby isn't cute. He's certainly that, though in a somewhat generic way. Like his apartment, Bobby has the kind of gloss that lacks character. He's the kind of attractive Frankie finds dull. Frankie watches him shuffle around the kitchen, a room he clearly isn't as comfortable in as one with more mirrors. He catches Frankie watching him and blushes, "Shut up. I'm a takeout queen, and I won't be judged for it."

"Oh, you're being judged," Frankie teases, taking the coffee cup from the brewer.

"Here," Bobby says, pointing to the refrigerator. "There's milk, cream, half and half, soy, coconut, almond. Sugar next to the stove. Agave. Stevia. Monk fruit powder."

"Oh, you're definitely being judged," Frankie adds, getting cream and sugar but still recalling how his dad refers to anything other than black java as "lady coffee."

Bobby leans against the doorway with his arms crossed. Frankie glances at him, taking note of the obliques peeking over his boxer-dog boxer briefs. Frankie sucks in his gut a little. Bobby may be bland, but he's still an audience.

Bobby seems to sense a shift in Frankie and smiles. "Does last night mean I can legally sexually harass you at work?

Could definitely make lunches more interesting."

Frankie laughs. "That it could."

Bobby does a little victory dance, and Frankie flashes to Hugo doing the same dance in the skywalk. There's a pang of guilt in remembering his last exchange with Hugo, juxtaposed with the ego boost of knowing he's driven two men in two days to a victory dance.

Bobby excuses himself and disappears down the hall toward the bedroom, leaving Frankie to survey the magnets and photographs on the refrigerator door. There's something familiar about the corner of a photograph, and he slides things around to get a better look. When he liberates it, Frankie feels both amused and ashamed.

"Damn," he mumbles. "I am one hell of an idiot."

"Yeah, you are," Bobby says, reentering the kitchen while sliding a T-shirt over his head. "You're an idiot for not knowing how bad I wanted you. It felt obvious."

Frankie hands him the photograph off the fridge. In it, Bobby is wearing a knit cap and laughing while playfully fighting off a kiss from a man who looks suspiciously like Hugo. Bobby looks at the photograph and chokes on a response.

Frankie shakes his head. "It was you."

"No, you've got it all wrong." The way the word sounds coming out of his mouth reminds Frankie of one too many conversations with Shane, and the way a spotlight becomes a gas light.

"Yes, it was," Frankie insists, tapping the stupid hat propped on Bobby's head in the picture. "My mother knit that cap for Shane, and he lost it. Probably up your ass."

Bobby is pale, wide-eyed, and mouth agape. "Let me explain."

Frankie gives him the stage, waiting, but Bobby falters, so Frankie takes it back, turning to pour the shitty coffee down the drain and rinsing out the mug as he recaps. "Hugo told me he caught his ex with Shane. In the break-up that followed, Hugo's ex told his family it was Hugo who had cheated, which, correct me if I'm wrong, is the same stunt you pulled with me at the Brians' wedding."

He turns to Bobby, waiting for a correction as he dries the coffee mug and returns it to the cupboard. When Bobby still hasn't said anything, Frankie points past Bobby, indicating that he should get out of the doorway between the kitchen and his exit. Bobby obliges, taking several steps back into the hallway. Frankie moves by him toward the living room, hoping like hell his shoes are in an obvious spot.

Bobby follows him into the living room and indicates where Frankie's shoes are tucked into a cubby by the front door. He knows better than to try to stop him from leaving. Frankie grabs his shoes and sits in a chair as Bobby stands nearby. He has to untie and retie them to get them on, so God knows how he got them off last night. The superpower of drunken sex, apparently. Add a reminder to buy slip-ons. As he works to get his shoes on, Frankie glances at the tattoo on Bobby's calf that he first noticed at the wedding, and a sudden smack of recognition knocks him backward. That wasn't the first time he saw Bobby's tattoo, and Bobby seems to realize it.

"I didn't think you saw me," he says, with the audacity of tears in his eyes.

"I didn't either," Frankie says, but he remembers so clearly now the tattoo on the legs wrapped around Shane's waist. "I guess I was so focused on getting my stuff out of the bathroom that I didn't pay attention to the piece of shit on the bedroom floor."

Bobby drops his head and sinks into the ugliest sofa Frankie has ever seen, whispering, "I'm sorry."

Frankie sits back with a calmness he hasn't felt in a while. Maybe seven months. Maybe 40 years. Shoes tied and ready to go, Frankie slaps his knees and stands up, sending Bobby flinching backward, which, truth be told, makes Frankie a little happy. Bobby struggles to make eye contact with him, keeping his eyes on a stupid cow print throw folded neatly in front of a faux fireplace.

"My mom left my father a few months ago. Maybe Shane told you that while his dick was in your mouth?" Frankie smiles at the way this makes Bobby shrink a little bit more.

"A few days before she left, she was at my house, helping me pick paint colors for the bedroom I was too stupid to realize wouldn't be my bedroom for much longer. Out of nowhere, she says, 'Sometimes I feel like I misplaced my life, and I need to find it while it's still of use to me.' "

Bobby glances up at him, wondering what this has to do with him, clueless to the fact that he's already become irrelevant.

"Isn't that something?" Frankie continues, shaking his head. "She told me she was leaving, and I was too focused on a future that wasn't mine to hear her. ... And ya know what color we picked? 'Rock bottom.' How's that for a kick in the cooter?"

He sighs, realizing his work here is done, and reaches for the door to leave, pausing to say, "Oh, and if it wasn't clear, I quit."

As he exits out the front of Bobby's apartment building, Frankie is relieved to recognize the East Village neighborhood and find his car waiting for him a couple blocks away outside Nowhere Bar. As he gets into his van, it is almost surreal how good Frankie suddenly feels, especially given the epic mess he has made of things. But he will fix what he can since he'll have to live with the rest.

And to do that, he has to get on with it, so he does.

31

CHRISTMAS.

THE SUN IS JUST starting to tease the morning when Clayton wakes up on Mona's recliner. She isn't in the chair across from him, but the pile of blankets indicates she was. He considers looking for her to say goodbye but decides against it. He leaves a note on the kitchen counter to thank her and quietly slips out of the house.

Back in his truck, he takes a leisurely long route home. It will be a busy day, and he needs a few extra minutes to himself. It's in these quiet moments along the back roads and gravel that, for the first time, he lets himself question whether or not the day will end with Carol by his side. He's confident that she's on her way now. Of course, she's coming back to them, back to him. But he also recognizes the uncertainty she brings alongside the trinkets and T-shirts and tales of travels far and wide because even when she's back, it never quite feels like she's back for good. He wishes his love and their life could be enough, but maybe it's not, and maybe it's time to let that be okay. He's reminded of something his mother said once as she was packing for her first trip abroad after Clayton's father died. Clayton was trying to warn her of how crazy the idea of this trip was. Carol busied herself in the kitchen, not wanting to add to the tension already in the room.

"Goddamn it!" Clayton's mother finally burst out, startling Clayton, who had rarely heard his mother raise her voice and had certainly never heard her curse.

She took Clayton's hands and patted his face, her eyes fiery with affection and intention. "I love you, son. But this is my time. I feel like I've lost my life and must find it while it's still of use to me."

In that moment, Clayton saw his mother differently. The woman in front of him wasn't just his mother anymore; she was a person with her own story that didn't revolve around him. For the first time, he realized the best way to love her was to let her go.

The hard part, he remembers, was redefining how he fit into her life. For so long, he had assumed it was his job to take care of her, to protect her. He had clung to a picture of what being a mother and son meant—a comforting, if idealized, fantasy. But now she was asking him to set aside that fantasy and make peace with a new reality: His mother needed to find herself, and he needed to respect that, even if it meant letting go of the role he had always known.

Turning into the driveway, Clayton is pulled back to the very real present where he finds an unexpected flurry of activity on the farm. The quiet solitude he had anticipated is replaced with a scene bursting with life and color. Neighbors wave to him as Christmas lights are being strung meticulously from the roof of the barn, their twinkling reflections dancing across the early afternoon sun. Plastic bells are being hoisted above the awning over the door, their bright red and green clashing cheerfully against the weathered wood of the farmhouse.

For a moment, Clayton just sits in his truck, his hands still gripping the wheel as he takes it all in. His heart, heavy with the weight of the morning's doubts, lightens at the sights around the farm. He had let himself consider the possibility that Carol might not return, which only felt foolish now in the shadow of an inflated snowman standing proudly in the middle of the lawn, its wide, grinning face against the backdrop of the summer greenery the only assurance he needed.

Matches and JP are the first to greet him as he steps out of the truck. Matches hands him a mug of coffee as JP thrusts an open box of curious-looking muffins in his direction.

"I made 'em," JP says, his cheeks flushing with pride.

Clayton accepts one and looks around, waiting for an explanation, not that he needs one. JP eventually breaks the silence. "We wanted to make sure everything looked right for Mrs. Parker."

Clayton's heart clenches at the boy's words, and for a moment, he can't speak. He reaches out, rustling JP's hair affectionately before pulling Matches into a hug.

"Thank you," he says, his voice thick with emotion.

The sound of a car pulling into the drive grabs his attention, and he turns to see an SUV he doesn't recognize.

His heart jumps with anticipation that this is Carol returning, jumping out to tell everyone they've done too much already and then commandeering them to do even more.

Instead, Frankie climbs out of the driver's seat and crosses to him like a dog with his tail between his legs, the viciousness of the previous night hanging in the air. "Hi, Dad," he says.

"Son," Clayton responds. "New car?"

Frankie nods. "It will be. I borrowed it for a couple of days to make sure it's right. The van is at the café."

They stand in silence, watching the neighbors laughing and chatting as they work, their shared energy transforming the farm into a festive wonderland. "Mom's gonna love this," Frankie says. Clayton feels him glance in his direction, hoping that this apology is enough. And it is. For now.

"I think she will," Clayton says, patting his son on the back and heading toward the house to get ready.

32

MESSY.

FROM THE KITCHEN WINDOW, Jules watches her father talking to Frankie. Frankie showed up in a new car, so maybe that means the enormous stick up his ass is starting to dissolve, though who knows, given the antics of the night before and the fact that neither of them showed up here last night.

After leaving the hotel, Jules drove by her house and considered forcing herself in, forcing Damon to hear her, to forgive her, to love her. Instead, she sat in her truck across the street and watched the lights in the house indicate Damon's activity. Sophie's light clicked off, then the kitchen light. Moments later, the light in the bathroom stayed on for the inordinate amount of time Damon spends brushing his teeth. She watched his shadow move through the living room to click on the small light they keep lit by the bookshelf. She ducked to make herself invisible inside a giant, obvious truck. The front porch light clicked off and she wondered if he noticed her or if he cared that she was stalking the life that had been hers mere hours before. She stayed in the truck until the bedroom light clicked off and the house disappeared into the shadows. She then drove out to the farm, stopping only for gas station pizza and beer. It had healed the broken heart of a 22-year-old when Joshua had left for the airport, but now it only tasted like regret. Delicious regret, but regret, nonetheless.

Watching her dad walk toward the house now, she wonders if it's appropriate to ask him where he spent the night. It all feels so unfamiliar. Frankie going AWOL isn't surprising, but her dad? Leaving in a huff after the fight with Frankie and with Mona in tow? It is easier for her to hope he'd been arrested and spent the night in jail than to consider any other option.

As her father comes inside and slips off his boots to put on his house shoes, she decides the best course of action is to pretend she doesn't know he's been missing all night. "I just got here," she says, a little too forcefully. He looks at her like she's transparent, but she just goes with it.

"Looks good, huh?" she says, nodding toward the outside, and he joins her by the sink, watching the neighbors stretch a string of lights across the chicken coop, ignoring the evil birds who peck at their feet.

She glances over at him, and he looks sturdy, confident, and strong. She wonders if perhaps some of that can rub off on her, and she leans her head against his shoulder. "I think I messed up."

She turns her head up to him to find him nodding.

"I'm sure you did. So, fix it."

She sighs at his assuredness as much as his confidence in her ability to mess up. Her father, always looking at life in black and white, makes it sound so simple. "I'm not sure I can."

"One way to find out," he says and kisses her on top of the head before heading toward the stairs. She watches him go and turns back to the window, but a picture of her mother tacked on the cabinet above the sink catches her eye. The glass of the frame glares from the morning light, and Jules finds she can shift her focus from seeing her mother's eyes to seeing her own in the reflection. They look so much alike in many ways, but she definitely has her father's eyes. For some reason, this brings her a sense of hope.

Her phone vibrates on the counter, breaking her reverie. She turns it over to see a text from Joshua: *Can I see you before we head out?*

She clicks away from the message to the screensaver of Damon and Sophie in balloon hats and wide, silly smiles. Jules takes a deep breath, feeling the weight of her choices. She knows she needs to address her own mess before facing her family, but she's got to give things time to relax. You can't see the extent of the damage from the middle of the storm. You gotta wait for things to settle.

The screen door slams as Frankie comes inside. Jules hears him slipping out of his shoes and into his house slippers. He walks through the kitchen but doesn't seem to notice Jules or, if he does, chooses to ignore her. So, she waits until she hears him finish his ascent up the creaking wooden steps and then follows him.

Maybe making him feel worse will make her feel better.

33

CARS.

"THIS IS THE SECOND DAY in a row that you look like a walk of shame."

Jules is standing in the doorway of Frankie's room. He's been here less than three minutes, and she is already taunting him. Where did she come from? She's exhausting. But brilliant.

"I had something I had to do," he tells her.

She is also relentless. "Something or someone?"

She gives him a wide-eyed leer that makes him laugh. It's impossible to keep it to himself anymore, so he tells her about Bobby. With each new detail, her eyes and mouth get wider. When she has cursed enough times to make a trucker blush, she asks, "What are you going to do about Hugo?"

His quiet reaction tips her off, and she slaps his knee. "I mean, what did you ALREADY DO about Hugo?"

He scrunches up his nose, shaking his head, imagining

Hugo's reaction when he returns to show Shane's house again. This time, he won't find a weird man sleeping in the living room. Instead, he'll discover the bucket of matchbox cars from the garage now spelling "Sorry" across the floor.

It's probably not enough to mend the bridge he burned between them, but maybe. He doesn't tell Jules about this ridiculous gesture, saying, "There's nothing to tell. Yet."

Jules doesn't believe him, but she doesn't push for details. Instead, she says, "Whatever it was, I hope it works."

In the silence that follows, something happens between them, an unspoken S.O.S. that they both recognize, both remember from times throughout their lives when the breaking was so near the surface that it was unfair to pretend otherwise. He pulls her into a hug.

"Stress hug," he whispers into the top of her hair. They started this as kids. They squeeze each other tight, holding it for several seconds until they both feel dizzy from not being able to breathe. But at least they feel something new.

He releases her and goes to his closet, wondering what to wear on a day built on so much uncertainty. Why do overalls feel weirdly appropriate? Because you can wear them to wade through the mud and muck life has dropped in your path? He pulls the overalls from the hanger, the denim stiff but familiar. There's something about their weight that feels grounding, like they could anchor him amid all this uncertainty.

He glances at Jules, holding them up. She shrugs. "Worse choices have been made lately."

It's a loaded comment, so he asks, "Wanna talk about it?"

"Not yet."

He waits to ensure she doesn't have more to say and then

looks back at the overalls. "Imagine Mom's reaction if I was wearing these when she walked in."

They let it sit out there, the shared doubts and fears. "Imagine," Jules says in a way that lets him know she's thinking the same thing. *What if she does show up?* When she'd been gone for six weeks, which was two weeks longer than any previous trip, they both voiced their concerns that this time might be different. This time might be for real. It's now been seven months. They'd both told themselves they'd made peace with the fact that she probably wasn't coming back, letting their father wallow in the delusion that she would return, but what if he's right?

He slides the overalls back into the closet and decides on something more appropriate, just in case: the army green linen pants and a cotton collared short-sleeve shirt that he wore to the previous summer's family reunion. Shoes would have to be decided after a very long, very hot shower. He could still smell Bobby's cologne and lies on his skin and he's hoping to send it all and so much more down the drain.

He sets the clothes on the bed and turns to Jules, who is shaking the plastic Magic 8 Ball they put far too much faith in as a child. She glances at him, daring him to ask what they both know her question was. When the answer settles, she grunts and hands it to him.

"Better not tell you now."

Tired of the games of the universe, he slides open the broken screen on the window above the desk and hurls the stupid ball out into the world. He feels Jules rush to his side to watch with him as it arches high in the sky. "Oh shit," they say in unison, moments before it bounces off the roof of Matches's pickup. The loud "clang" gets the attention of everyone outside, and Frankie and Jules pull back to either side of the desk.

Frankie peeks outside to find Matches standing in the middle of the yard with her hands on her hips, looking directly at him. "Franklin Everett Parker!"

He pulls Jules down as if it matters , and they laugh together while crouched on the floor.

"Ow, my knees," he whines and settles off his haunches to sit on the floor, and Jules follows suit.

As their laughter settles, they both feel the return of angst, which he decides to ward off in the only way he knows how. With shock therapy.

"You're fired," he says, and her eyes snap up to his with a startled gasp.

"Are you serious?"

"Well, demoted anyway." He nods. "It's time I got back to my real job, my real life."

"Okay, thanks," she says, wiping away fresh tears he feels have nothing to do with his return to work. "I have so much to figure out."

Then she looks toward the open window. "Sure wish I had a Magic 8 Ball right about now."

34

OPENING.

THE SUN HAS NEARLY given up on this Sunday. It waves goodbye from behind the rolling hills, blowing kisses across the cornfields to anyone who might be paying attention. Clayton is standing at the kitchen sink, refusing to make eye contact with the moon. It's already high in the sky, daring dreamers to make wishes that may never come true. That's the risk of wanting. Sometimes you get what you want, and sometimes you get what you need.

Clayton is not sure he's got the strength to wish anymore. Sixty-five years have taught him enough to know that a wish is not a frivolous notion. It's a reminder of the wanting and the loss and the wonder. These are not things a wise man takes lightly. Neither should a fool. And Clayton is once again wondering if he's more foolish than wise.

He washes the coffee mug again. It couldn't be cleaner than if it were fresh from the dishwasher—which it is—but he rinses it off, anyway. Then he notices which coffee mug he's holding, whose coffee mug he's holding. It's old and brittle, with small chips in the green and white spotted glaze. Frankie made it in third grade. It's not exactly a work of art, but it does the job. And it's here.

Unlike her.

For a moment, he considers throwing the mug to the floor, and the burst of rage surprises him. To everyone else, what happened this afternoon or, more precisely, what didn't happen, makes sense. He wants it to make sense, and maybe soon it will. But not yet.

He sighs and gives in with a glance at the moon, cursing the call to wish. Nope. Not gonna do it.

Instead, he straightens his tie and looks around the kitchen for some new distraction. Realizing the distraction itself has become distracting, he pours a healthy splash of whiskey into the coffee mug and takes a sip. Maybe the burning in his throat will torch all the questions that refuse to be still.

She didn't show up.

This time, she's gone.

He again rinses the mug and flips it upside down onto the windowsill to rest next to the glamorous, lumpy twin Jules had made for Clayton. He stares at the mug, remembering how he'd discovered Carol's note in this exact spot seven months ago. He was too exhausted by his confusion to even miss her. The exhaustion was deeper than physical; it was a weariness of the soul, a slow erosion of the foundation on which he had built his life. The idea of missing her felt abstract and distant, like trying to mourn something that was never fully his to begin with. This realization, that she had always been leaving, even when she was here, and he had always been waiting, brought with it a strange, hollow clarity. Who would he be if he stopped waiting?

He let go of the counter and straightened up, the kitchen around him coming back into focus. The familiar surroundings seemed different now. He didn't have all the answers—he wasn't sure he even wanted them yet—but he knew one thing: He couldn't keep waiting. Not anymore.

The low hum of Frankie and Jules talking pulls him to the doorway between the kitchen and the dining room. Frankie sees him first and stops speaking, cueing Jules to cut her sentence short. She peeks over her shoulder at her father and smiles like you do when your insides are breaking. Clayton wants to catch her and save her, though that feels pointless when it's pretty clear that all three of them are falling. They're falling together, at least, so that's something. And maybe they're not falling apart. Maybe they're falling in place.

Frankie has managed to strip a wine bottle fully of its label. It's now doing naked pirouettes on the table, sent spinning by a flick of Frankie's wrist. Jules catches the bottle before it makes a suicidal leap to the hardwood floor. The moment reminds Clayton how different his children are. Frankie would have thrown ten thousand mugs to the floor by now. Jules would have picked up the most promising casualties and glued them back together. This has always been their way. Frankie explodes, and Jules rebuilds.

A beam of light moves across the walls as a car pulls into the driveway, accompanied by the rustle of gravel. There's a collective gasp in the room.

Both children look up at their father with wide, teary eyes. Clayton can't look at them. Not yet. He clears his throat and runs his hand over his tie as he steps from the kitchen and moves toward the front door.

"Dad," Jules says, choking on the word. Clayton looks back at his children, who have come to stand in the dining room doorway. Jules the rebuilder, Frankie the destroyer.

"I know," he says in response to their silent screams. "I know but just give me one more minute to believe."

He takes a deep breath and straightens his tie one last time before going to the door. He hears a car door open and close, followed by footsteps on the path. He waits a moment longer and then opens the door.

His eyes are cast down and closed as he takes a moment to let the truth settle into his skin. It doesn't feel great, but acceptance rarely does. But it also hurts a little bit less than expected. And that is a lovely surprise.

Clayton finally looks up. He has tears in his eyes, but he knows he will be okay.

They are all going to be okay.

"Hello."

EPILOGUE

Closure.

It was Christmastime when she found herself back in town. She hadn't intended to return, but she had fallen asleep while her friend drove. She didn't let on that she knew this place far too well.

It felt cruel to be here. Her heart threatened to rip through her chest as they turned the final corner and stopped out front of the little coffee shop by the sculpture park A handwritten sign hung on the door, "Closed for a private party."

"They're not open," her friend says.

She had pretended to search for a place to eat, feigning spontaneity, but she knew exactly where she was leading them. Here. After hours. Where she expected to find an empty café, not to confront what she had left behind.

Funny thing about expectations—how they hold you together, right up until the moment they break you apart.

She saw Jules first. Her hair was longer now, falling over her shoulders. She had let her bangs grow out and tucked them behind her ear, likely pinned in place with a twist tie pulled off a bag of bread in a last-minute fix. Jules moved through the café, carrying plates to a small group tucked off to one side.

A younger man moved to the side, and she saw Frankie

laughing beside him. He looked good. She glanced around for Shane and the boys but didn't see them. Maybe they were at home? Frankie's hand rested on the chair where the unfamiliar young man was sitting, and his thumb gently rubbed the back of this man, who turned to wink at Frankie. Oh, so maybe Shane was finally past tense.

A moment later, Damon walked out from the kitchen carrying Sophie, who herself was carrying a cake lit with candles. Even from the car across the street, she could hear a boisterous rendition of "Happy Birthday" begin, loud and off-key, as nature intended.

When Clayton stepped out from the kitchen behind Damon, she felt herself gasp. He was beautiful with time, wearing a kitchen apron and juggling several wine glasses and two bottles of wine, all while singing along at the top of his lungs. When he reached the table, everyone shifted enough for her to see Mona Falcone beaming with joy as the cake was set before her. Clayton leaned down to whisper something in her ear, and it shattered her in ways she knew she deserved. He wasn't hers anymore. That she knew. What she hadn't planned on was how it would feel to realize she was no longer his.

Mona Falcone. Of course. That made sense.

She wondered what would happen if she walked over now. What could she possibly say to explain something that was never meant to happen—how a question became a choice, how she didn't realize she was leaving until she was already gone?

Maybe someday she'll be able to explain.

But not today.

She watched Clayton, Frankie, and Jules, and their joy resembles peace. That's not hers to take away.

She wiped away a tear, cleared her throat, and turned back to the road ahead.

"We should keep going," she said.

And they did.

THANK YOU

This story began as a screenplay that spent years gathering dust. During a particularly tough time at the start of the pandemic, I needed something creative to distract me from daily life, so I decided to turn those pages into a novel. The first draft came quickly, but then it struggled under the weight of doubts and excuses.

The finish line of sharing only happened through the kindness, generosity, and guidance of so many wonderful people.

So Thank You …

To Jill East, with whom I co-authored my first book in 2nd grade.

To Sarah Mihalec Maloney, who was the first person to champion this story.

To Christine Riccelli, Teri Vannoy, Jon Roemer, Nicole Frail, and Jay Blotcher for your sharp eyes, honest feedback, and belief in the story's potential.

To Tim Johnson, Mellisa Nichols, and Michelle Baker for

your thoughtful insights, encouraging words, and willingness to sit with rough pages. Your support helped me keep going when it would've been easier to stop.

To the ones who distracted me from the work in the best possible way: Nick Bertelsen, Aimee Francis, Erik Hastings, Dan McCarthy, Sarah Noll Wilson, Heather Paris, Amy Pettinger, Kim Petrallia, Caprice Ridgeway, Danielle Taddei, and Karin Tucker.

To Shelley Watkins, for the rom-coms, the pub crawls, and the porch swing daydreams.

To Drew McLellan and the AMI family, for embracing my curious mind with a place to play.

To Jolene Pfaff, whose belief in me reminds me to believe in myself.

To Niki Lewin, for the quiet place to think.

To Tim Prough, for making this book *look* as good as I hope it *reads*. And for the music.

To my sister, Julie Gonzalez, for reminding me to moo at the cows.

To Tony & Estella Marquez, who expanded my family.

To Dave Marquez, who brought film noir, soft clothes, and comfortable joy into my life.

To my mother, Anne Hodina. You are missed.

And of course, I must thank you—you big, bad, beautiful dreamer.

Cheers, Weirdos.

About the Author

Shadley Grei wrote his first story in second grade and has been chasing words ever since. He lives in West Des Moines, Iowa, with his husband, too many books, and never quite enough time to read. *Before Closure* is his first novel.